God's Will Be Done

Kirk decided to risk a long shot. "Are you aware that in four days this planet will encounter a black hole—and be destroyed?"

Domo's jaw dropped. "You are a terrible liar," he said.

"No," said Kirk, deliberately calm. "My ship possesses certain instruments which allow us to see ahead."

Domo snorted. "Another lie. If such were truly the case, Ay-nab would have told me long ago."

"Then you'd better ask him—and soon. My ship is a large vessel. I'm willing to take all of your people on board to save their lives. I can't do it now. I'm trapped here. If you or Ay-nab knows how to set my ship free, for your own sakes, tell me."

Domo fidgeted on the stool. "We are fated to die because of our misdeeds. What you are suggesting is a terrible blasphemy." He looked up at Kirk. "No one can violate the will of a god."

Bantam Spectra Star Trek books
Be sure to ask your bookseller for the titles you have missed

STAR TREK: THE CLASSIC EPISODES, VOLUME 1 by
James Blish and J. A. Lawrence
STAR TREK: THE CLASSIC EPISODES, VOLUME 2 by
James Blish
STAR TREK: THE CLASSIC EPISODES, VOLUME 3 by
James Blish and J. A. Lawrence

THE PRICE OF THE PHOENIX by Sondra Marshak and
Myrna Culbreath

THE STARLESS WORLD by Gordon Eklund

THE STARLESS WORLD

GORDON EKLUND

BANTAM BOOKS

NEW YORK • TORONTO • LONDON • SYDNEY • AUCKLAND

THE STARLESS WORLD
A Bantam Book published under exclusive license from
Paramount Pictures the trademark owner.
Bantam edition / November 1978
Bantam reissue / March 1994

For information address: Bantam Books.

ISBN 0-553-24675-5

Published simultaneously in the United States and Canada

Bantam Books are published by Bantam Books, a division of
Bantam Doubleday Dell Publishing Group, Inc. Its trademark,
consisting of the words "Bantam Books," and the portrayal of a
rooster, is Registered in U.S. Patent and Trademark Office and in
other countries. Marca Registrada. Bantam Books, 1540 Broad-
way, New York, New York 10036.

PRINTED IN THE UNITED STATES OF AMERICA

RAD   0 9 8 7 6 5

1

Captain's Log, Stardate 6527.5:

The awesome spectacle of the Galactic Core continues to weave a spell over the ship's crew, even those veterans who've passed this way before. For me, the hushed atmosphere aboard ship is more nerve-racking than relaxing; I'm accustomed to the steady hum of constant activity. So far, a total of fifty-seven black holes have been charted. It's my guess that the proximity of these mysterious objects plays a major role in the mood of the crew. As for our assigned mission, evidence continues to be negative. We're apparently alone here in the Core. There's been no sign of Klingon activity.

With a soft cushion of air supporting the back of his head, Captain James T. Kirk of the USS *Enterprise* lay on his bunk, his eyes fixed to the rectangular screen at the foot of the bed, where a stream of words zipped past at a velocity faster than the average eye could follow. Still, Kirk's eyes were better than average, and he was easily able to read what the ship's computer quoted for him, the text of an old novel, one that Chekov, his navigator had originally recommended to him: *War and Peace* by the nineteenth-century Russian Leo Tolstoy. This was Kirk's third visit to Tolstoy's by-now-familiar world of philosophers and saints, noblemen and peasants, lovers and soldiers, sinners and statesmen. Mr. Spock, his Vulcan first officer, whose knowledge of Terran literature was immense, rated *War and Peace* among the three greatest novels composed by human beings, while Chekov emotionally insisted that it was by far the best of them all. For Kirk, who seldom had time to read for pleasure, the wonder of the book lay in its ability to assume and then transcend the trappings of mere reality. While reading, he had trouble convincing himself that this was only a story: the characters and the world they inhabited were more real to him than the room he occupied. At the moment, totally engrossed, he followed Pierre, one of the protagonists of the book, as he wandered through the ruins of devastated Moscow in the wake of Napoleon's invading army.

Then, without warning, the world of Tolstoy vanished from the screen, and Kirk found himself gazing upon the impassive visage of Mr. Spock. "Captain Kirk, I apologize for the interruption, but something odd has come up."

Although he knew Spock wouldn't invade his privacy without sufficient cause, Kirk couldn't help a measure of irritation from creeping into his tone. "What's wrong now, Mr. Spock?"

"It's a Federation shuttlecraft, Captain. The sensors detected its approach some time ago, and further investigation revealed that the craft is occupied. There appears to be only one man aboard."

Totally returned to the world of the present—nineteenth-century Moscow far away—Kirk shook his head. "That hardly seems possible, Mr. Spock. There are no Federation starships within several hundred parsecs of our present position. Shuttlecraft do not operate independently."

"I am aware of that, Captain, and requested computer identification. The shuttlecraft is one of the complement of the USS *Rickover*."

"The *Rickover*?" said Kirk, letting his eyebrows

rise slightly in surprise. "The *Rickover* was lost more than twenty years ago."

"How general?"

"Eleven light-years."

"That's a lengthy jaunt for a shuttlecraft. You said there was a man on board. Have you attempted to contact him?"

"Communication was established some time ago. I had no wish to disturb you until all necessary data were on hand."

"And?" said Kirk, irritation returning to his tone.

Spock's cautious nature sometimes grated on his nerves.

The pilot replied to my transmission. He wished permission to rendezvous with the *Enterprise*."

"Did he identify himself?"

"He gave a name."

"Did you check it with the *Rickover's* last roster?"

"The name would not have appeared."

"How can you be so sure of that?"

"The name was not unfamiliar to me."

Kirk glared at the face on the screen. "And what was that name, Mr. Spock?" he said with exaggerated patience.

"The pilot told me his name was Jesus Christ."

"Oh," said Kirk. "Then I assume that he isn't—he couldn't stifle a smile—"he isn't the famous one." But could he be sure? The presence here of a lone shuttlecraft was unlikely enough. When that shuttlecraft turned out to belong to a starship lost twenty years ago, it wasn't just unlikely; it was impossible. Jesus Christ? Unlikely, surely—but impossible?

"The computer, as well as my personal visual analysis, indicates that he is not."

"Then the man is, I assume, mentally unstable."

"That appears to be true. His speech indicates a

high degree of stress. Dr. McCoy has gone to the shuttlecraft bay to await rendezvous."

"When will that be?"

"In approximately five minutes, ship's time."

"You did wait till the last moment before calling me."

"I felt there was nothing I couldn't handle," Spock said stiffly.

"No, of course not," Kirk said quickly. Has he inadvertently wounded Spock's pride? "I think I'll join Bones below. I've always wanted to meet the Son of God."

"As you wish, Captain."

"And, Mr. Spock, one other thing. I want to thank you for not disturbing me until it was necessary. You handled the situation well."

"It was the only logical course to pursue."

"Ah, yes . . . naturally, it was."

Kirk let the screen stay blank. After Spock's call, there was no way he could return to the mood of Tolstoy's stable, cloistered, unambiguous world of Russia before the great revolution.

2

As Captain Kirk approached the shuttlecraft bay, he heard the voices of struggling men not far ahead. Quickening his pace, he turned a corner and saw a thin, skull-faced man of uncertain age writhing in the grasp of two security men. A fourth man, Dr. Leonard McCoy, the ship's chief medical officer, circled the other three like a cat stalking its prey. McCoy held the butt of an air-powered hypodermic in one hand.

The thin man kept shouting, "Fools, release me! I am the prophet! I am the messenger of the one true god!"

McCoy, despite the assistance of the security men, couldn't quite seem to sneak close enough to strike home with his hypo.

"Stop this!" Kirk shouted, using his most commanding tone. "Stop this at once!"

The security men, recognizing the voice of their captain, immediately froze. More surprisingly, so did the thin man. A contented smile spread across his face. His eyes were like saucers. "At last," he said. "A man capable of recognizing the truth."

Dr. McCoy frowned, keeping his hypo poised. "The man isn't rational, Jim. He's got to be calmed down."

"Why? What happened? Did you say something to upset him?"

"I told him he wasn't Jesus Christ and he jumped at my throat."

"Maybe he knows more than we do." Kirk looked closely at the man. There was something familiar about him. Puzzled, Kirk stepped nearer.

"Careful," said McCoy. "There's no telling what he may do."

Kirk gazed straight at the man's face. He was too old and too thin. His clothes were torn and ragged, and his body stank. "Thomas?" Kirk said tentatively. "Thomas Clayton?"

The man's head jerked suddenly. He grinned at Kirk, showing missing teeth. "I am known by that name."

"Do you remember me? Do you know who I am?"

"You're Jim Kirk, of course." His tone was as blank as his face.

"Thomas, I thought you were dead . . . long dead."

"I am dead." Suddenly he giggled. "Isn't that the point? I am dead, and yet, because of Ay-nab, I live again."

"Thomas, what's happened to you?"

But Clayton was laughing. His whole body shook, but barely a sound emerged.

Kirk nodded silently to McCoy, who took a quick leap forward and brought the hypo down against Clayton's arm. Clayton went stiff for a second. His mouth worked up and down, but he couldn't make a sound. He collapsed in the arms of the security men.

"Take him to sick bay," McCoy said. "Tell Nurse Chapel I said to put him in a private cell."

"Yes, sir."

As the men turned away, McCoy looked quizzically at Kirk. "What's the problem, Jim? You look as though you've seen a ghost."

"Maybe I have. That man is Thomas Clayton. He and I were roommates at the Academy my first two years."

"That wasn't a Star Fleet uniform he was wearing."

"Thomas washed out."

"Oh," said McCoy. "What happened?"

"It was a desperation move, I think." Kirk's voice softened. He was recalling another time, when he was barely more than a boy. "I never met his family, but they were all he'd talk about. The adult men were Star Fleet clear back to the creation of the Federation, and way before that, a number were famous sailors in the navies of Earth. You know what I'm talking about, Bones. Thomas felt he was nothing more than the most recent bearer of a grand tradition. He was never a very good student. He was bright and clever—probably too clever. If a particular course didn't interest him, he'd flunk it. We took an exobiology course together. It was required for graduation. Thomas did poorly. He knew a lot about computers. He tapped one and obtained the answers to the final exam."

"And got caught," McCoy said.

"I turned him in."

McCoy looked hard at Kirk. "Star Fleet Academy and its rigid code of honor."

"It serves a purpose."

"He was your friend."

"It's not that simple. For a while, I felt the same way, but Thomas stole the exam, not me. I gave him every chance to confess. What sort of officer would a cheater make?"

"A pretty poor one." McCoy shook his head. "All right, Jim, I get your point. When it comes to honor, I won't attempt to lecture you. Still, none of this explains what Clayton is doing here aboard a shuttle-craft belonging to a long-lost ship."

"All I know about Thomas Clayton is that he went into the interstellar trading business. He did well—as clever as he was, he should have—and was wealthier than any dozen Star Fleet captains. About five solar years ago, he vanished in space. He was alone aboard his own ship. There was a search, but it's a big Galaxy."

"Was he lost near here?"

"I think so. I think he was headed in the direction of the Core."

"Then that would explain it."

"Some of it, Bones." Kirk shook his head. "Not much of it."

"It's curious."

"Yes, isn't it?" Kirk was thinking of the vista of tightly packed stars he had seen on the viewscreen. The trouble with the Core was its scale; it was too vast—a man felt petty by comparison. "I'm going to join Spock on the bridge. When Clayton comes around, call me. I'll want to question him."

"It might be another twelve hours. More, considering his physical condition."

"Call me whenever."

"Sure, Jim. Good luck."

Kirk wasn't sure what McCoy meant by those final two words, but he appreciated them. Luck—that was what a man needed to thrive in this universe. It changed the scale. A star couldn't have good luck—a planet couldn't. That took something alive and conscious, something like a man.

With that reassuring thought on his mind, Kirk rode the turbolift toward the bridge.

3

Captain's Log, Stardate 6528.4:

Our mysterious guest, Thomas Clayton, has now been awake and alert for nine hours. I have twice visited his cell in sick bay in hopes of getting him to shed some light on the reasons for his presence here. Unfortunately, on both occasions he refused to respond to direct questioning. When asked to explain his whereabouts since his reported disappearance, he either ignored the question or else spoke of different matters entirely. For the most part, Clayton raves like the worst imaginable religious fanatic. He insists that he is the chosen son or favored prophet of a deity named Ay-nab. According to him, the human race (my assumption; his actual phrase is "the people") will be destroyed in the very near future. I've tried to get him to explain what makes him so sure, but he just ignored me and went on spouting nonsense as before.

A couple times, he did make better sense. He admitted owning and operating an interstellar trading ship. He told me the terror he had felt while adrift in the void. Unfortunately, when I asked him to elucidate, he went on to describe how he was rescued by the passage of Ay-nab and went to dwell in the paradise of Lyra under the watchful eye of the god. He said nothing concerning the USS *Rickover* or how he came to be in possession of one of its shuttlecraft.

As a result of these conversations, I've decided to

9

leave Clayton under the personal care of Dr. McCoy, hoping he may grow more lucid with the passage of time. If not, when we leave the Core, Clayton will be committed to Starbase 13, where the psycho-computers may be able to unravel his story.

"That's odd," Lieutenant Sulu said from his helmsman's seat on the bridge. He studied the flickering screen in front of him. "That's damned odd indeed."

"A problem, Lieutenant?" said Captain Kirk. He slipped out of his command chair and stood behind Sulu. As a captain, Kirk made it a habit to ignore nothing odd that happened on the bridge of his ship.

"Something I ought to know about?"

"That's hard to say, sir." Sulu indicated the viewscreen. "Two hours ago, the sensors detected a stellar-sized object almost directly ahead. I tried a visual scan, couldn't see anything, and naturally assumed it was another black hole. I asked for additional data, but these figures have nothing in common with a black hole."

Kirk bent down to examine the symbols on the screen. "No, they certainly don't. There's light in the visual spectrum. That's impossible for a black hole. It must be a dwarf star on the verge of extinction."

Sulu tapped the screen. "With a diameter of three hundred million kilometers?"

"No star that big could be invisible at this distance."

"That's why I thought it might be a rogue planet."

Kirk shook his head. "It's way too big for that. Do you have a density reading?"

"That's something else that's odd. The sensors can't seem to come up with a firm figure."

"Why not?"

"The computer says there's a paradox."

"What?"

"It won't tell me. I think it's embarrassed."

Mr. Spock, returning from an inspection tour of the enlisted quarters, stepped off the turbolift. Kirk waved to him. "Mr. Spock, we have a problem maybe you can help with."

Spock leaned past Sulu's shoulder, studying the data on the screen. "There's no figure here for density."

Sulu explained why this was so.

"Odd," said Spock. He stood, facing Kirk. "It could be a protostar."

"I've thought of that," Kirk said.

"It doesn't explain the problem with the density reading."

"That's what bothers me."

Ensign Chekov, the ship's navigator, who occupied a chair to the right of Sulu, let out a sudden cry of alarm. "Captain Kirk, Mr. Spock, there's a divergence in our course."

Kirk glared at the man seated in front of him. "Lieutenant Sulu, now what's going on?"

Sulu's fingers danced across the control panel. "Sir, it's true. I can't seem . . ." He appeared to be battling the controls.

Spock went over and stood beside Chekov's chair, studying the navigational data that showed on the console. With a finger, Spock drew a line across a starmap of the Galactic Core. "I believe this is the way we're presently heading."

A tight knot of tension settled in Kirk's stomach. He looked at the starmap and Spock's pointing finger. "Is it significant, Mr. Spock?"

"It may well be, Captain. If my memory is correct, our altered course will intersect the object we were just discussing."

"We are being drawn toward it?"

"That is a possibility."

"By what?"

"By no natural force within my sphere of knowledge." Spock crossed to the library/computer station, his usual post on the bridge. Leaning forward, he murmured a request for data.

Kirk knew the only sensible thing for him to do was wait for Spock to come up with a logical explanation for what was occurring. Returning to his command chair, he sat down and, using the intercom, called the ship's engine room. The worried face of Lieutenant Commander Montgomery Scott, chief engineer of the *Enterprise*, materialized on the viewscreen.

"Scotty," said Kirk, "I want you to disengage the engines at once, cut all power. We seem to be in the grip of—"

"That's just not possible, Captain," said Scott excitedly. His Scottish accent seemed even thicker than usual. "Velocity is increasing. There's nothing we can do."

"I gave no such order, Mr. Scott."

"I know that, sir. No one did. The engines revved up on their own. We can't stop them."

"That's impossible, Scotty."

"I know that, too, Captain. It's almost as if an outside force had crept in here and taken control of the ship."

4

Thomas Clayton awoke in the darkness of his cell in sick bay. One moment he swam in the depths of dreamless sleep; the next, he was alert and sitting up.

He had heard a voice. Ay-nab, the one true god, had called to him.

"Yes, Majesty," Clayton whispered. He understood the danger if he spoke too loudly; the monitoring device Dr. McCoy had concealed in the room might overhear. "I feel you near me, Lord."

Clayton listened intently. When Ay-nab spoke, no such primitive instrument as language was necessary. Clayton heard the voice of his god. He understood fully.

"I am coming," he said softly. "I will obey your divine command." Swiveling on the bed, he let a foot drop to the floor. He was tense, his skin bathed in cold sweat. Inside him, a struggle still raged. Clayton realized, no matter how dimly, the full import of what he was being forced to surrender: his freedom of will, his sense of humanity. Still, he was dead. Ay-nab had fed upon his soul for too many years, until nothing remained of the essence of life. The struggle inside him was unequal. A dead man matched against an all-powerful god. The result was never in doubt. When the one true god called, Thomas Clayton obeyed.

He stood, his movements jerky, and crossed the room. The cell was uncluttered. Except for his bunk, the only furnishings consisted of a soft plastic chair and table. Dr. McCoy had hidden his monitoring device in the shielded viewscreen in one wall.

Reaching the padded door, Clayton brought down his fists hard. He cried out, "Help! Help me! I'm dying! Can't anyone hear?"

Clayton wasn't dying. He felt fine.

"Help! Help me!" He pounded his fists. "Please help!"

At last, through the thick door, he heard muffled steps. One man only. McCoy, he hoped. If the doctor wasn't alone, his plan was ruined.

Kirk deserved the blame. He knew Kirk. Once, long ago, in a past that now seemed as distant as Andromeda, Kirk had betrayed him. In his ignorance, Kirk had also failed to heed the word of the true god. Still, he would learn. Clayton grinned. Soon enough, Jim Kirk would gaze upon the merciless yellow eye of the god.

The door opened. Stepping back, Clayton raised his hands against the blinding light that swept into the room. Fingers pressed his bare arm. A voice said, "Clayton, what in the name of—?"

He struck blindly. Eyes sealed, he lashed out with both fists. There was a cry. He felt the impact of bone against bone. Clayton forced open his eyes. He saw a figure—it was McCoy—reeling backward. There was blood on his face. Clayton swung again. He struck McCoy squarely on top of the head. McCoy tottered. His knees buckled. He fell, striking the floor firmly, rolling on his stomach.

Suddenly anxious, Clayton took hold of McCoy's wrists and dragged him into the cell. He shut the door and stood in the corridor for a long moment, watching and listening. In his white pajamas, he stuck out like a painted pony. He should have taken McCoy's uniform. Why hadn't his god counseled him?

That was blasphemy. Ay-nab would surely see him through. Reaching his destination would require the stealth and cunning of a wild beast. Ay-nab would not want it to be too easy.

Clayton moved down the corridor. Closed doors stood flush with the walls. Clayton always knew when there was danger ahead, when to stop and wait and hide. Ay-nab guided him. Clayton ran, stopped, trotted, ran full-tilt again. It should not have been possible for one man to maneuver safely through the innards of a ship containing more than four hundred crew members. Clayton did it—with ease.

Where was he headed? So far, the god had not confided in him. Did it matter? He moved effortlessly through the heart of the great ship. Distantly he heard the muffled roar of giant engines. He slipped past open doors. From some, he heard fragments of conversation. *Ship off course. Mystery planet. Engine room's lost all control. Collision course.* He sensed the anxiety, the dread of the speakers. These people understood the might of a god. Kirk, too, in turn, would be taught to believe.

He rode a turbolift upward. Voices reached him from close ahead—taut and edgy with concern. He smiled, recognizing Kirk's voice among them. Poor Jim. Jim the Betrayer. Won't you know soon enough?

The turbolift stopped.

Clayton stepped out.

"Hey, you! Mister! What do you . . . ?"

He recognized the bridge. He should be here himself. There. In the command chair. Captain Thomas Clayton. He saw Kirk. A creature with green skin and pointy ears—Vulcan half-breed. Two men at the helm. A black woman.

The woman had shouted at him.

Clayton edged deeper into the room.

The others had seen him now. Kirk was halfway out of his seat. The Vulcan pointed a finger like a schoolmaster disciplining a student.

Clayton moved calmly forward.

"Thomas, get away from there! You can't . . ."

He had seen the screen. Above the helmsman's chair. A big wide rectangular viewscreen. And on it, reflected brilliantly, the hidden face of the one true god.

Kirk caught his arm. "Thomas, sit down. What do you want? What's wrong?"

Clayton brushed past him.

He stood beneath the screen.

He looked up, placed his hands under his chin, locked the fingers in a tight fist, fell to his knees. "My god," he murmured. "I cower before you. As you bid, I have done. These ignorant ones gaze upon your sacred eye. Forgive my sins. Ignore my life. I am your servant. You are the master."

The viewscreen showed, among the stars, the smooth black disk of a lone planet. *My god*, thought Clayton. *My lord.*

5

Mr. Spock, chief science officer and second-in-command of the Federation starship *Enterprise*, devoutly believed that only the Vulcan discipline of logic offered a successful means by which to confront the mysteries of the cosmos. Although his mother was a native of Earth, Spock was more the son of his father, a fullborn Vulcan.

Less than five centuries ago, the people of Vulcan had barely avoided self-extinction as the result of a series of intraspecies wars, and in the wake of that disaster, the Vulcans had developed their system of disciplined logic, which had once and for all eliminated the curse of a barbaric heritage.

If Spock could have been granted one wish, he would have asked to see the discipline of logic extended to encompass all the civilized planets of the Galaxy.

But the act of wishing was in itself illogical. There were other problems—practical problems—confronting him, and for these, the discipline of logic usually served well.

Still, the difficulty with the problems presently facing the *Enterprise*—the mysterious object ahead, the loss of ship's control, the appearance of Thomas Clayton—was their steadfast refusal to be solved by logical means. For Spock, this did not necessarily indicate that the discipline of logic had failed. On the contrary, he believed that the failure must lie either with the quantity and quality of the data at hand or else with his own reasoning processes.

Spock stood on the bridge, anticipating the return of Captain Kirk from sick bay, where he had gone to deliver the escaped prisoner, Clayton. Spock had devoted several minutes of concentrated thought to an attempt to uncover some logical explanation for Clayton's behavior, but in the end he had been forced to admit that any explanation depended upon one as-yet-unknown factor: the sanity of Clayton himself. The actions and motivations of any genuinely mad man stood forever beyond logical analysis. Logic prevailed in balance with a sane and orderly universe. When madness held sway, logic was rendered quite useless. Still, though some men were mad, the universe itself was not. That, in fact, was the key.

As he awaited Kirk's return, Spock went to the library/computer station and reviewed the latest sensor data concerning the odd world toward which they were now heading. One particularly interesting factor was the extremely reflective surface of the world. The sensors, interpreting the raw data received, had arrived at a tentative conclusion. The surface of the planet, assuming that it was a planet, had to be as smooth as a ball.

Captain Kirk, when Spock first informed him of this conclusion, had expressed dismay. "That's ridiculous, Mr. Spock. No amount of surface erosion can explain such a thing. Have the sensors take another reading. There must be some mistake."

"Not necessarily, Captain," Spock had said, adopting what was, for him, a diplomatic tone. Captain Kirk unfortunately suffered from a tendency to spring to hasty conclusions. For a human being, Kirk possessed an extraordinarily logical mind. Nonetheless, he often relied too heavily upon intuition. "There is a logical explanation for the analysis. The planet may be an artificial construct."

"But, Spock, this thing is huge, bigger than Jupiter. For any civilization to have created such a world would make them as superior to us technologically as we are to a tribe of gorillas."

Spock nodded tightly, unable to recognize a contradiction. "The possibility of such a society is not illogical, especially considering that the *Enterprise* has lately come under the control of an undetectable force."

"Then you think whatever this force is, it originates on this world."

"That seems probable, especially if this world is a created object."

"You're talking about an incredibly big starship."

"A rather large one, yes," Spock said dryly. The word "incredible" was not normally part of his vocabulary. There is another factor that also tends to confirm my thesis. I don't believe you've seen this before." He showed Kirk a section of the sensor readout. "It appears that the radiation which first led us to believe that the object was a star actually emanates only from a relatively small surface area. What we're talking about is a circle no more than a few hundred kilometers in diameter."

"But a world can't be part planet and part star," Kirk said.

"It can be, Captain, if that small area is what I think it may be: an opening in the surface of the globe."

Kirk frowned. "And the radiation?"

"The radiation is actually emanating from inside the sphere. It is my present opinion that what we have here is a hollow planet with a small star located in the center."

Kirk nodded slowly. "I thought that's where you might be heading. A Dyson sphere."

"Named, as you no doubt are aware, for the mid-twentieth-century scientist who first theorized their existence. All the planetary matter of a solar system wrapped around the dying central sun. A means for preserving supercivilizations in their extreme old age."

"But Dyson spheres are strictly theoretical. None has ever been discovered before."

Spock shrugged. "Then perhaps we are the first."

"You really believe this, Spock? This is definitely your opinion?" Kirk cocked his head to one side, like a cautious bird of prey uncertain whether to strike.

"It is the one logical conclusion," Spock said.

And nothing Spock had learned in the intervening two hours since that conversation had altered his opinion. The approaching planet now showed clearly on the central viewscreen, a huge black orb, its surface features, if any, totally obscured by a pinpoint of brilliant white light shining from the northeastern hemisphere. This, Spock was convinced, was indeed a Dyson sphere, and he was eagerly anticipating the prospect of visiting such a marvelous construct. And he would be visiting it, too. There was no longer any remnant of doubt. The *Enterprise* was headed directly toward the world.

Captain Kirk, returning to the bridge, stepped off the turbolift, glanced briefly at the viewscreen, then settled down heavily in his command chair. Spock sensed that Kirk was upset, but still there were important matters to discuss. If their present course and velocity remained unchanged, they were due to collide with the Dyson world in less than two hours.

Spock left the library/computer station and went to stand beside Kirk's chair. "I assume that Dr. McCoy's injuries were not serious," he said.

Kirk shook his head, glancing quickly up, as if startled to discover that he was not alone. "He took a pretty rough knock on the head. Slight concussion. He'll be fine in a day or two."

"I'm pleased to hear that. And the prisoner? Thomas Clayton?"

"I had Nurse Chapel give him a strong sedative. He ought to be out for the next several hours. Before that, I tried to question him. It was as hopeless as ever. I . . ." Kirk paused. It was obvious to Spock that Kirk had noticed some of the same things about Clayton's recent actions that Spock himself had. "When Thomas was here on the bridge, did you make any sense out of what he did?"

"'Sense' may not be the proper term, Captain. The man does seem to be definitely deranged."

"That may well be, but even a madman's world, though distorted, isn't entirely unreal. Did you notice where he went?"

Spock thought that was what Kirk had in mind. "To the viewscreen. He appeared to be . . . worshiping it."

"The screen?" said Kirk.

"Or what was on it."

"The planet?"

"It seems conceivable that Clayton may have come from there."

Kirk nodded. "That would explain how he managed to be aboard a shuttlecraft way out here."

"But not how the shuttlecraft itself came to be present."

"True," said Kirk. "In fact, there are a great many things we're a long way from explaining. Still . . ." He glanced at the viewscreen. "I have a distinct feeling that place there contains a great many of the answers we're seeking, about Clayton, about a lot of things. I'm assuming, of course, we aren't about to be smashed to bits against the surface of the planet."

"That was something I wished to bring to your attention. During your absence, Mr. Chekov reported a slight alteration in our course. We now appear to be headed toward the opening in the globe."

"Then we are going inside." Kirk shrugged. "I suppose that's not surprising. If whoever's running this show wanted us dead, with its apparent power there would be swifter ways than a planetary collision."

Spock nodded. This was exactly the point he'd wished to get across. He stepped back. "Any further instructions, Captain?"

Kirk swiveled slowly in his chair. "I'm afraid not, Mr. Spock. The power to give instructions is out of my hands at the moment. We wait. Wait and see what happens next. That's the best I can offer in the way of advice."

6

"Pellucidar," said Dr. Leonard McCoy. His arms folded across the chest of his blue uniform shirt, McCoy stood tensely on the bridge to the left of Captain Kirk's chair. Like everyone else, he was watching the central viewscreen, where the dark orb of the approaching planet stood outlined against the even darker void of deep space.

"What was that, Bones?" said Kirk.

"A name that just popped into my head," McCoy said. "It comes from a book I read as a child." The top of his head was bandaged. His upper lip and the bridge of his nose were bruised. "Pellucidar was supposedly the inner world of Earth. Upside down. There was a normal world on the outer crust, with Pellucidar hidden underneath."

"A physical impossibility," Mr. Spock put in. He stood to the right of Kirk. "For example, there would be no source of internal light, and besides—"

"The author supplied Pellucidar with its own inner sun," McCoy said. "That's what brought it to my mind." He indicated a portion of the viewscreen where a blinding light shone. "From now on, for me at least, this place is Pellucidar."

"The natives may have their own name," Kirk said.

23

"If there are any natives."

"Someone brought us here."

"Or something."

Conversation on the bridge had been sporadic all along. The communications officer, Lieutenant Uhura, had transmitted a signal through the gap in the surface of the planet, but no response had been received. The sensors continued to scan the approaching world, but none of the new data proved especially consequential. Kirk had retained some hope that the sensors might discover the nature of the force that presently controlled the ship. Like so much else, this too remained a mystery.

Kirk continued to watch the viewscreen as the bright hole in the face of the planet grew wider. "It's a perfect circle," he said, in obvious wonder. "An incredible engineering achievement."

"I wonder how thick that crust is," McCoy said.

"I intend to make a measurement as we pass through," Spock said. "Since the purpose of such a world is to maximize surface area, I imagine it's as thin as possible."

Because of the fact that the planet now filled the entire viewscreen, a subtle shift in orientation occurred among all those present. The planet became a fixed point of reference; they were now traveling in a downward direction.

"Look at the size of that thing," Ensign Chekov said excitedly from his console. "It must be a fantastic sight to see in there."

"I'm not sure any of us is capable of imagining such a scale," Kirk said. "The surface area must be equal to that of a medium-sized star. Fully inhabited, a planet that size could support a population number-ing into the trillions. There would be room in there for every intelligent creature in the Federation—room to spare."

"What I don't understand," Dr. McCoy said, "is why anyone should bother. Population pressure really doesn't explain it. Neither does a dying sun. There's always space. An infinite number of worlds to colonize."

"Maybe the natives just like this place better," Chekov said.

"Then they'd have to be pretty damn simple."

"There is another explanation, Bones," said Kirk. "Perhaps space wasn't open to them. Perhaps they never discovered the warp drive."

"With a technology capable of building their own planet?" McCoy shook his head. "Personally, I like Chekov's suggestion better than that."

"On your own planet, Earth," Spock put in, "several highly advanced societies—the Inca people of South America, for example—never discovered the secret of the wheel."

Kirk fully understood how useless such speculation could be, but he made no attempt to turn the attention of his officers to more practical matters. In fact, he found it difficult to keep from joining in himself.

"I think we're going through," Lieutenant Sulu suddenly said.

Kirk glanced up at the screen. The gap had grown enormously since the last time he'd looked. Beyond it, Kirk thought he could almost make out the shimmering sphere of the inner sun. The Enterprise was falling at a rapid velocity. "Switch the screens to a side view," he ordered. "The light ahead's too bright to be of much use."

Almost immediately the viewscreen showed a split transmission. For a brief moment the packed stars of the Core glowed brightly. Then the Enterprise slipped inside the gap. The sides of the hole seemed smooth and slick. Kirk could have pinched himself. This might have been a dream.

Mr. Spock studied his wrist chronometer.

"What are you doing?" Kirk asked, tearing his eyes away from the screen.

"I wanted to make my own estimate of the surface depth. This way, I can . . ."

Spock broke off. The viewscreen was showing another view. Rising up from below, the *Enterprise* glided past a circle of snow-tipped mountains. Kirk stared openmouthed at the screen. After a moment the mountains vanished. The screen showed a broad vista of blue sky and white clouds.

Spock looked at his wrist. "Fifteen kilometers." He reached past Kirk to the intercom. "I'll call Mr. Scott to confirm our relative velocity."

"Do that," said Kirk. He was watching the screen.

Spock spoke quickly and softly. He turned to Kirk. "My estimate is apparently correct."

"A crust only fifteen kilometers thick?"

"Yes, Captain."

"That's incredible."

"I don't know if I would use that exact term."

No, Kirk thought, I'm sure you wouldn't. Nonetheless, it was true. The surface area of this planet was even more immense than he had at first conceived. All the matter of a solar system—planets, satellites, comets, meteors—flattened out and formed into a hollow sphere. "Better switch the screens to show what's underneath. Now's as good a time as any to take a look at our new home."

The *Enterprise* had by now risen several kilometers above the ground, but the viewscreen picture still revealed only a limited view of what lay below. Kirk noted that the gap in the surface through which they had passed was barely visible, surrounded on all sides by high mountains. He saw ribbons of blue, probably rivers, and deep azure splotches, most likely lakes. The land nearest the mountains was gray-brown in color, while farther away, green predominated—forests and grasslands. At the right edge of the screen, he noticed a dark green blur that might indicate an ocean shore; the rivers seemed to be heading in that direction. Kirk realized this was only an infinitesimal slice of the whole world; to explore all of it thoroughly would consume several of Methuselah's lifetimes.

The *Enterprise* continued its steady ascent. The ocean showed clearly now, shaped in a perfect square. As the ship soared even higher, Kirk saw that this was part of a general pattern. The surface below was like an enormous curving chessboard, alternating squares of ocean and land. Kirk made no attempt to speculate on what might have motivated the builders to establish this particular design. It was neat, colorful, and functional. Although the large ocean areas did reduce the habitable landmass considerably, Kirk assumed that what remained was sufficient for its creators' purposes.

A flurry of activity gripped the bridge as the sensors relayed the first definite data from below. Kirk leaned back in his chair and waited patiently. Whatever was important would be brought to him in due time; he trusted the competency of his crew. Mr. Spock made frequent use of the library/computer. Sulu and Chekov studied their screens and charts. While he waited, Kirk contacted Scott twice. Both times he received the same report: the engines of the *Enterprise* continued to function independently; conscious control remained in the power of an unknown force.

Spock left his station and crossed to Kirk's side. He said, "I can give you a preliminary report on this planet, Captain."

"Start with the atmosphere," Kirk said. This was always the initial factor he preferred to consider.

"A nitrogen-oxygen balance. Pleasantly breathable. Surface pressure is also quite bearable."

"Gravity?"

"Earth normal."

Kirk shook his head. "Are you sure?"

Spock nodded. "I think it's artificially maintained."

"I see. Native life forms?"

"More than we can possibly analyze at this time. Land, air, and oceans are densely inhabited."

"Signs of civilization?"

Spock shook his head slowly. "None."

This was hardly the answer Kirk had expected. "Would you mind saying that again, Mr. Spock?"

"I was also rather taken aback and took a computer projection. There are two possibilities. Either the civilization that built this planet is so advanced that we cannot detect it, or else it has become extinct."

Kirk eyed his first officer curiously, but Spock, as usual, managed to conceal his emotions beneath the rigid mask of his face. "And your opinion, Mr. Spock?"

"I have none, Captain. Information is at present insufficient."

"There is a third possibility," Kirk said.

"Oh?" Spock raised his eyebrows in surprise.

"Maybe they're hiding from us—deliberately."

"That would require a force field. The sensors have detected nothing of the kind."

Kirk shrugged. "I'm only speculating, Mr. Spock." His eyes shifted to the viewscreen. It was never far from his mind—that amazing chessboard, now largely obscured by clouds. The *Enterprise* had climbed to an altitude of one hundred kilometers. The blue sky had turned dark.

"Sir," said Lieutenant Sulu, "I believe we've ceased to ascend. We appear to be going into orbit."

"Orbit?" Kirk left his chair. Spock followed him to Sulu's station.

"Around the inner sun, sir. We're like a trapped satellite."

"More correctly, a planet," said Spock. "We are orbiting the sun."

Kirk glanced at the viewscreen. From this height, with the covering of clouds, it was difficult to gauge. Still, he had no reason to doubt that their climb had ended.

"So now what do we do?" said Dr. McCoy. He had arrived on the bridge partway through the conversation. "You're not going to beam down a party, Jim?"

Kirk shook his head. "If I did, where would I send them?"

"Then we're trapped."

"Not necessarily. I've got to believe there's some purpose behind this. If we wait, something will eventually come along and explain."

"What?" said McCoy.

"The answer to that may be the most interesting of all."

"Captain Kirk?" It was Sulu. "The sensors have picked up an object directly in front of our present position. It's a ship, sir."

"Better give me a picture." Kirk, Spock, and McCoy observed the miniature viewscreen on the console in front of Sulu. Kirk studied the image of the ship reflected there. He smiled—without amusement. "Well, what do you know?" he said.

"A Klingon battlecruiser," said Spock.

"Well, there were reports of their presence in this area."

"It seems to be in orbit the same as us," Sulu said.

"Captain Kirk?" It was Lieutenant Uhura.

He turned away from the screen. "Yes, what is it?"

"I'm receiving a transmission, sir."

"From below?" Kirk said eagerly.

"No, sir, I don't think so. The language is Klingonese."

7

Captain's Log, Stardate 6532.3:

I have now ordered an end to yellow-alert status and an immediate return to normal duty, as it has become increasingly apparent that the Klingon battle-cruiser that precedes us in orbit fails to possess the ability to transform the threats of its crew into action. To confirm my evaluation, I ordered an engineering analysis of our own weapons system and discovered that the ship's phasers were no longer functional. I assume that the same force that continues to control the ship has also chosen to render us—and the Klingons—weaponless.

James Kirk leaned back in the soft cushion of his command chair and half-consciously raised his hands and rubbed his eyes with his knuckles. He knew he was tired and needed to rest, but so much had been happening these past few hours there had been no opportunity for escaping the bridge, even for a moment. He started to yawn but quickly stifled that, glancing across the width of the bridge to where Dr. McCoy, his head still bandaged, was peering back at him with an expression of intense concern. Kirk smiled sheepishly and shrugged, ignoring McCoy's unspoken admonition. In another hour or two Spock would return, and then he could go and get all the rest he needed.

"Find anything yet, Uhura?" he asked in his most

authoritative tone, more for the benefit of McCoy than anything. He turned his chair toward the library/computer station, where the slim, dark-skinned communications officer worked in her red uniform dress and high black boots. Uhura and McCoy were the only officers presently on the bridge. Kirk had sent the others below after ordering an end to the yellow alert.

"I'm continuing to scan the surface," Uhura said, "but there's still nothing. Every conceivable variety of life form, but nothing indicating intelligence. If the Klingons are down there, though, I know I'll find them."

"How much of the surface have you actually scanned?"

"Less than ten percent, I'm afraid."

"Does that include the oceans?"

"No, sir, it doesn't. I just hope, though I've tried to be thorough, that I haven't missed anything. It's so huge. Finding something as minute as an individual power transmission is like looking for a needle hidden in a haystack. That's the right expression, isn't it? A needle in a haystack."

"That's it," Kirk said with a smile, "but haven't you ever wondered, Uhura? What's the needle doing in the haystack in the first place? Why would anyone put it there? For that matter, why would anyone want to find it? It seems to me it would be easier just to go out and buy a new one."

"Maybe the farmer was snowed in," McCoy suggested, "and couldn't get to a store. It was the only needle he had, and there was a big hole in the seat of his pants."

"How do you know we're talking about a farmer?"

McCoy pointed to his forehead. "The discipline of logic," he said with a wink. "Who except a farmer, would have a haystack around?"

"But the needle wouldn't belong to the farmer," Uhura said. "It would be the farmer's wife. Remember, we're talking about times when the roles of men and women were severely restricted. In fact, that's what I don't understand. Any decent farmer's wife would know enough to keep a supply of needles always on hand."

"Maybe the farmer was a bachelor."

"Or a widower. She could have died."

"Frozen to death. In the snow."

"Or he killed her."

"With the needle."

"Sure, that's why he hid it."

Kirk shook his head. The fact that this conversation hadn't struck him as immediately silly was just an indication of how really tired he must be. Lieutenant Uhura and Dr. McCoy went solemnly on with their discussion. Grinning, Kirk turned in his chair. The Klingons he suspected of being present on the surface of the planet could wait. Everybody deserved a few minutes' break.

Kirk had received the distinct impression that something untoward was afoot when, accepting the initial Klingon transmission, he had discovered the smooth face of a junior officer glaring back at him from the viewscreen. Where was the Captain? Although the young officer made a valiant effort to be as crude and abusive as any more experienced Klingon, Kirk's suspicions were not eased. The young officer threatened to destroy the *Enterprise* unless Kirk immediately surrendered his ship and crew. When Kirk asked why he should, the Klingon answered with a colorful stream of invective, which the translator dutifully rendered into universal terms. Kirk took the precaution of ordering a yellow alert, then delivered his own pungent reply. When, several hours later, nothing had happened, Kirk decided to return the Klingon's call.

The same junior officer, his features contorted by an expression of deep loathing, appeared on the viewscreen.

Kirk grinned broadly. (He often found it difficult to regard the humorless Klingons with all due seriousness.) "We're still here," he said. "I thought you promised to burn us out of the sky."

The Klingon tightened his lips, then started to unloose a chorus of cursing.

Kirk, impatient with the game, cut him off. "I demand to speak to your commanding officer," he said.

The Klingon for a brief moment looked worried, but soon recovered his composure. "My captain is not available to the likes of you."

"He'd better make himself available or I'm apt to burn his ship his ship out of the sky."

"Threats, idle threats," the Klingon said mockingly.

Now, look who's talking, thought Kirk. His actual words were more direct. "I am James Kirk, commanding officer of the USS *Enterprise*, and I demand to speak to my equal."

"You have no equals aboard this ship, Earther. Only superiors."

"I'd still prefer talking to someone old enough to shave." The young Klingon, unlike many of his race, was beardless. Kirk didn't know if this was because of youth or personal preference, but from the glare he received in reply, he guessed he must have struck a nerve. "Are you sure your captain's on board?"

The Klingon was flustered now. "Of course he is. Where else could he possibly be? He's on board, but he refuses to converse with you."

"He might possibly have beamed below."

"There is no life on that world. It is of no concern to the Federation. You must surrender. We have claimed title to this planet in the name of the Klingon Empire."

Kirk had heard enough. He had no idea of what the hell was going on, but of one fact he was certain: the Klingon captain would indeed be found below.

A short time after that conversation, Kirk ordered Mr. Spock to begin a kilometer by kilometer sensor scan of the planetary surface. When Spock's duty watch ended, Kirk asked Lieutenant Uhura to take his place.

He felt a hand on his shoulder and realized he had come dangerously close to nodding off. It was McCoy. "Jim," the doctor said, "I've got to go down to sick bay. Why don't you come with me and grab a nap? Uhura can call if anything happens."

"How is Clayton, anyway?" Kirk said, struggling against his fatigue. He couldn't leave Uhura alone on the bridge, and it was too early to call Spock.

"He's locked up good and tight, if that's what you mean." McCoy touched his bandages. "I've got a medic watching him every second."

"I was more concerned with what he might be saying." Kirk leaned back and stretched his legs. "I'm convinced he's lived on this planet. If we could get him to talk lucidly, it might save an awful lot of effort and time."

"I can't offer much hope there, Jim. I've tried everything short of shock treatments. If anything, I'd say his condition has worsened since his escape. If you want, come with me and talk with him yourself."

Kirk shook his head, smiling inwardly. He knew this was just another of McCoy's ploys to get him below. "I think I'll stick it out here for the time being."

"Jim, are you sure that's wise?" McCoy said, gazing straight at him.

Kirk turned totally serious. "I appreciate your concern, Bones, but I'm quite able to gauge my own resources."

McCoy looked skeptical but didn't argue. He was no doubt aware that where the safety of his crew was concerned, Kirk took few risks.

McCoy stepped aboard the turbolift and with a wave vanished below.

Kirk turned back to the viewscreen, where the chessboard surface of the planet continued to flow past. The cloud cover seemed especially thin at this point, but there was a wide patch of darkness covering one entire corner of the screen. It was nighttime. One fact the sensors had uncovered was the presence of an even dozen moons orbiting the planet at altitudes ranging from one hundred to eight hundred thousand kilometers. These moons were so positioned that they frequently passed directly in front of the sun, and the resultant eclipses provided the planet with the only form of night that it possessed. To Kirk, this was simply further evidence of the incredible engineering talents of the original builders. The moons, like the planet they served, were undoubtedly artificial constructs.

"Captain Kirk," Lieutenant Uhura said suddenly, "I think I've got it."

His fatigue ebbing at the possibility of success, Kirk hurried to the library/computer station. "The Klingons?"

"I believe so, sir. I'm getting definite evidence of electronic activity, probably a communicator of some type. I've ordered a closer scan of the area, and . . . Wait, here it is now."

Uhura leaned close to the console. After a moment she rose, smiling. "It's confirmed, sir. Bipedal life forms. I can't be certain they're Klingons yet, but it does seem likely."

"How many?"

She checked the console again. "Fifty. At least that many."

"That sounds like an awfully large landing party. Still . . . I want you to pinpoint that exact location for later transport. I'll contact Mr. Spock. Now we can go below."

"Me, too, Captain?" Uhura said tentatively.

Kirk half-turned. "Aren't you tired?"

"No more than you, sir."

"I plan to catch a nap before we beam down."

"Then I can, too. After all the time I've spent scanning this planet, I'd hate to lose the chance to see it firsthand."

Kirk smiled. "No, I suppose not. Okay, Lieutenant,

I'll add your name to my list. Take three hours. We won't beam down before then. Pinpoint the Klingon location, then grab a nap."

"Thank you, sir," she said, matching his smile.

As Kirk stepped aboard the turbolift, he was already mentally composing the probable makeup of the landing party. Himself, of course, and Lieutenant Uhura. Sulu? Yes, he'd want someone who knew how to handle a phaser. McCoy? No, not Bones—he wasn't fully healthy yet. Nurse Chapel, then. Spock would have to remain aboard the *Enterprise*. Because of the Klingon ship, Kirk wanted to leave an experienced man in command. Scott, too, would have to stay behind—in case something else happened to the engines. The four of them would have to do, then. Four, plus a couple of security men. Klingons were not noted for their friendly ways.

Kirk whistled happily as he knocked on the door to Spock's quarters. He was making things happen now, no longer standing obliviously aside and letting them happen to him. It was better this way—and more fun, too.

8

Dr. Leonard McCoy placed his hand upon the lock that held the thick cell door shut and waited as it slid slowly open. Taking a step forward, McCoy peered cautiously into the bright room beyond. When his own eyes confirmed the monitor's report that the patient, Thomas Clayton, was fast asleep, he turned and waved at the stockily built young medic who stood across the corridor. "It looks all right, but keep your ears open. I ought to be out in ten minutes."

"Yes, sir," the medic said.

McCoy moved stealthily into the room. The door cycled silently shut behind him. McCoy headed toward the bed.

He had gone only a short distance when he discovered that the monitor was no longer correct in at least one respect: Clayton was not asleep. His eyes were open, and he was watching McCoy.

"Well, hello," McCoy said glibly. "Feeling any better?" He stopped beside the bed and looked down. Something in Clayton's expression reassured him, something that seemed nearly sane.

"I feel like . . . like I've passed through hell and come out the other side."

"In a manner of speaking, maybe you have."

37

McCoy reached down and grabbed hold of Clayton's unresisting wrist. He counted the pulse, found it normal, then felt his forehead. "Know where you are?" he asked in his best bedside manner.

"Sure. On a ship. The *Enterprise*, isn't it?" He spoke slowly, as if each word required a tremendous expense of energy.

"It is indeed. Know who I am?"

"You're a . . . a doctor."

"Leonard McCoy. Ship's chief medical officer."

"Then, if you're a doctor, maybe you can tell me something."

"Be glad to. Here . . . let me join you." McCoy drew up a soft plastic chair. "What is it you want to know?"

"It's about me—my condition. Am I . . . am I dead?"

McCoy stared questioningly at Clayton, but the man seemed to be entirely serious. "From a medical viewpoint, you're alive. You breathe, your heart beats, you can think and talk. I don't know what else there is."

"What if it's not . . . not me who does it? What if something else does all that?"

"Like who?" said McCoy.

"Ay-nab."

McCoy nodded gently. He wanted to draw Clayton away from his delusions, not plunge him back into the middle of them. "What about you?" he asked. "We've all been wondering how you came to be here."

"I escaped. Didn't I tell you that before? There's always been that one shuttlecraft around. He destroyed all the other ships, but kept that one. I don't know why. I'd tried it before. This time it worked, so I took off."

"Then you did come from that planet, from the Dyson sphere?"

"Yes, from Lyra."

McCoy frowned. "I wanted to call it Pellucidar. Is that the natives' name? Lyra?"

"It's his name—Ay-nab's. You see, I took off in the shuttle, but I knew all the time he had to be laughing at me. I was dead. Where could I go? Still, I found the crown of mountains. I passed through the gap. I wasn't afraid. I knew I couldn't go far in a shuttle-craft. I had no provisions, not even water, I didn't care. I was dead already. What did it matter? Then I saw your ship. I called. You responded. I actually thought I was saved."

McCoy was uncertain how to proceed. How much of the truth should he reveal to Clayton? He decided to move in stages—a bit of the truth at a time. "When we picked you up—I don't know how much you remember—you acted very uncommunicative."

"I acted crazy," Clayton said unhesitantly. He laughed sharply. "What did you expect from a dead man?"

McCoy was determined to ignore Clayton's apparent obsession with his own death. Couldn't the man even tell when he was alive? "You were ill," he suggested.

"I am sorry about hitting you," Clayton said.

"I've been hit harder. You weren't responsible for your own actions."

Clayton nodded eagerly. "No, it wasn't me—that was him. I wanted to be sure you understood that. As soon as I reached the Enterprise, he started to talk to me. What could I do? He wouldn't let up. His voice was as loud as an explosion. I couldn't even think. I had to do what he said."

McCoy tried to express the obvious question in a matter-of-fact way. "Who is this person who talked to you?"

"Why, Ay-nab, of course. The . . . the god."

"Of Pellucidar? Lyra?"

"Sure."

"He lives there?"

"No . . . not exactly."

"But he's real, correct? I mean, you can see him and talk to him. You're not just talking about a spirit."

Clayton laughed. It went on too long and grew too loud. He seemed on the verge of losing control; then suddenly he was calm again. "Oh, no, he's real enough. You can see him. He's right there every day, and on Lyra we hardly ever have night." He looked around the room, as if seeking someone who ought to be present. "But where's Kirk? Jim Kirk? I know I remember seeing him here."

McCoy saw no reason not to reply. "Captain Kirk and a landing party have beamed down to the surface of Lyra. That's why we could use your help. If you've actually lived there, you may know a lot of things that are still mysteries to us. For instance, what—?"

Clayton was laughing again. He interrupted. "Down to the surface of Lyra? Now, isn't that funny? Poor Kirk. He'll find out all he needs to know soon enough. There's no way out of here, Doctor. Do you understand? No way out at all."

"What are you talking about?" McCoy leaned forward, unable to disguise his anger. If Clayton knew anything definite, it was his duty to speak. Old animosities shouldn't be permitted to endanger the lives of innocent men and women.

"Talking about? Talking? Talk?" Clayton's voice rose hysterically. "I'm doing a lot more than talking, Dr. McCoy. You wait. You just wait. Pellucidar, you call it? Well, don't fear the planet. Look to the star. That's where you'll see the truth. That's where you'll glimpse the mighty eye of the god. Drop to your knees. Hide your eyes. Cower. Whimper. Wail. Grovel in the dirt like a worm. Gaze upon the divine countenance of the one true god on high and listen to the word that. . . ."

McCoy stood slowly, backing away. Clayton went right on speaking, a stream of unquenchable words.

Clayton was back in his own private world once again.

Opening the inside lock with his handprint, McCoy stepped into the corridor. The medic, hearing Clayton's excited voice through the open door, hurried across the corridor. "Sedative," McCoy said. "Just a half-dose. Don't knock him out. Let the poor bastard rest."

"Yes, sir."

As he waited for the medic to finish, McCoy wondered if he ought to notify Kirk of what Clayton had said, the possibility of danger below. It wasn't really necessary, he finally decided. Any landing party was always alert to the possibility of unexpected trouble. And Clayton had never really said anything specific. He was a frightened, irrational man. Well, perhaps later. This first period of lucidity might be a sign of better times to come. The next time he might discover something more definite.

Something more definite, that is, if his own present diagnosis was correct, if Clayton really was a sick man. If something else was at fault, if Clayton was correct in his belief that an outside force had taken control of his mind, then recovery might be very far off indeed.

But that was ridiculous—wasn't it? What could this force possibly be? The same one that had taken control of the ship's engines and weapons? That was certainly an idea worth considering, but that was all it was. Just an idea. McCoy had no proof. Nothing worth sharing.

Inside the cell, Clayton's voice grew quiet. The medic reappeared and locked the cell door.

"I did as you ordered, Dr. McCoy."

"Fine. I think I'm going to take a turn on the bridge. While I'm gone, keep an eye on him. Check the monitor every few minutes. Anything happens, call me at once."

"Yes, Doctor."

McCoy rode the turbolift. He felt a jolt deep in

his stomach as the lift shifted direction, gliding up toward the bridge rather than sliding horizontally. What Clayton had said—the part about the god—had never really made sense. Perhaps that's what disturbed him the most. It was irrational, but not quite irrational enough to be easily dismissed. If not a god, then why not someone or something very powerful indeed? What? he asked himself. He shook his head. He didn't know. Clayton had said they'd all find out soon enough. Perhaps that advice was the best.

5

"This is nearly too perfect to be real," Kirk said, speaking as much to himself as anyone else. The six-member landing party from the *Enterprise* edged cautiously forward through the thin, sun-spangled forest where the transporter had dropped them. Kirk had positioned his people in a horizontal line, with each instructed to keep well in sight of whoever stood to the left. So far, such precautions had proved unwarranted. This was more than just a peaceful world. It was a veritable paradise. Ripe fruit hung in heavy bunches from the branches of nearly every tree they passed. The temperature was warm but not unpleasant; the wind was no more than a whispering breeze.

As he passed beneath the low branches of a squat tree, Kirk reached casually up and removed a round bright yellow fruit. Turning slightly, he tossed the fruit to his left, where Lieutenant Uhura made a graceful catch. "Run a tricorder analysis on that," he said. "Let's see if it's edible, too."

As she continued forward, Uhura worked the tricorder with practiced fingers. So far, every fruit they had checked, ranging from tiny red berries to huge melonlike pods, had proved deliciously edible. It had to be springtime, Kirk decided. A perpetual spring?

43

On a world such as this, true seasons would not likely exist.

"Not only edible, Captain Kirk," Uhura said, "but extremely nutritious. Want it back?"

He shook his head and patted his belly. "I think I ought to pass on this one. You have it."

She gazed longingly at the smooth-skinned fruit. "I'm supposed to be watching my weight. Here, with all this"—she waved her free hand at the surrounding trees—"that won't be easy."

Kirk grinned, moving around the broad girth of yet another fruit-laden tree. This one was more like a bush in appearance, with sharp thorns and a bounty of bright blue berries. He didn't ask Uhura for another tricorder analysis. Considering their previous results, that seemed superfluous.

Lieutenant Sulu moved directly to Kirk's right. Sulu, like Kirk, held his hand phaser in constant readiness, but this too seemed like an unnecessary precaution. Uhura's tricorder had so far turned up only one life form that might possibly be regarded as threatening, a bearlike carnivore that seemed common to these woods. The Klingons, if they were Klingons, remained several kilometers ahead. Kirk preferred this method. He could have beamed down in the middle of the Klingons if he'd wished, but he wanted to be sure the Klingons had time to evaluate his presence. Sudden surprise tended to produce a reaction of either anger or fear. A Klingon, whether frightened or angry, was not an easy creature to handle.

The sky above was a flat blue sheet, infrequently punctuated by bursts of white cloud. A tiny full moon stood poised at the tip of one horizon, which sloped upward here on this inner world, a phenomenon that would become more apparent once they'd left the obscuring thicket of the forest. Because of this moon, a brief moment of night would descend upon them in a few hours. Kirk expected to reach the Klingons well before then.

Suddenly, ahead in the low branches of a big-leafed tree, Kirk caught sight of the faintest flash of motion. He threw himself flat on the ground and thrust his phaser in front of him. "Get down!" he shouted. "I saw something! Drop!"

Kirk swiveled his head, saw no sign of his own party, then sighted down the length of his arm. They huddled close to the trunk of the tree. Kirk tried to count. One, two, three . . . maybe four. Because of the swaying leaves, he couldn't see clearly. Were they humans? Klingons? He couldn't be sure.

Keeping his phaser aimed at the tree, Kirk turned to Uhura, who lay on her stomach nearby. "Check your tricorder," he said in a soft, cautious voice. "See what they are."

"I already did. They're bipedal forms. Four of them. Standing on that big branch close to the trunk."

"Klingons?"

"No. They're less than a meter tall."

"How did you miss spotting them before?"

"That's what has me worried. I checked the tricorder ten minutes ago, and I swear there was nothing then, except one of those big carnivores, and he's still there."

"Where?"

"I was going to warn you. He's coming this way. Give him another two minutes. He may smell some-thing."

"Us?"

"Or them."

"What about them? Are they armed?"

"Apparently not. They're naked, for one thing."

"Then they're certainly not Klingons." Kirk smiled thinly. "A Klingon might shed his pants. He'd never go anywhere without his agonizer."

"I can't detect anything of the kind."

Kirk nodded. Without ever forming a conscious decision, he loosened his grip on the phaser and let it slip closer to the ground. Not humans, not Klingons. A local form of life, after all. Intelligent? That wasn't proven. There was only one sure way of finding out.

Kirk came to his feet. He slid his phaser into his belt and took a step forward. "Cover me," he told Uhura and Sulu. "I'm going to see what there is to see."

"Watch out for that carnivore," Uhura whispered.

"It's still coming?"

"Faster."

Kirk held his empty hands in front of him, a nearly universal gesture of good intentions. His eyes were fastened on the branch of the tree where he had first spotted the aliens. Through the leaves he saw something white. Skin? Fur? Uhura had said they were naked. As he came closer, he raised his voice.

"I come in peace and friendship." He kept his voice well-modulated. There wasn't a chance in a billion they could understand a word he said, but tone and pitch could be even more important.

The tree shook. A heavy object dropped to the ground. The tree shook again, and another object fell. Kirk stopped. There was a third and a fourth.

Kirk studied the creatures beneath the tree. They resembled plump chimpanzees, with white fur, flat nostrils, and bare faces. Three were males, but the fourth, several centimeters shorter than the others, was plainly a female.

"Stay back," Kirk warned his own people. "I think they're harmless enough. Watch me."

He took a tentative step forward. The aliens watched him, tense but not obviously afraid. He still couldn't be sure they were anything more than animals, but his instincts told him differently: these were intelligent beings.

He took another step.

Just then, there was a loud crashing in the forest to his right. He turned his head in time to see the big carnivore Uhura had warned him about come charging into the tiny clearing. It looked like a small grizzly bear, moving on all four feet. The aliens, seeing the beast, froze where they stood. Ignoring Kirk, the beast headed straight toward them. It stopped suddenly, rose on its hind legs, and stared, like a discriminating shopper in search of a good buy.

The aliens never made a sound. Their bare faces registered terror.

Kirk pointed his phaser at the beast and carefully squeezed.

Nothing happened.

He squeezed again.

Still, nothing. The phaser refused to respond.

Turning his head desperately, he saw Uhura and Sulu on their feet. Both had their phasers pointed at the beast, but in neither case did anything appear to be happening.

Just then, the beast finally made up its mind. It staggered forward on two feet, front paws extended. The female alien backed away. The beast came toward her. The other three aliens, the males, broke and ran. The beast ignored them. They disappeared into the forest.

Breaking her own spell, the female screamed. Her voice was shrill and high-pitched, like a human child's. She tried to run, but the tree was in her way. She turned with her back to the trunk. She screamed again.

The beast trudged toward her.

At the same moment, Kirk sprinted forward. He dropped his useless phaser and, a few steps later, grabbed a fallen branch of the ground. It was a big fat stick, perfect for a club. He screamed at the beast. It appeared not to hear him, concentrating on its prey.

Kirk arrived at the last possible moment. The beast raised a paw to swat the alien's head. Kirk struck first. Digging his heels into the soft dirt, he swung his stick. The blow struck the beast square in the back of the head. It noticed Kirk this time. With a roar it turned away from the alien and advanced on Kirk.

He felt absurdly defenseless. What was this? A lone man with a stick, standing against a beast nearly twice his height and four times his weight. "Get!" he shouted. "Get out of here! Hey! Move!"

He swung the stick again. As hard as he could. Straight at the beast's moist snout.

His blow struck home.

The beast roared.

Kirk knew it would now do one of two things: it would attack in a rage or run off in pain.

He stood his ground, stick poised to strike again.

Fortunately, the beast elected the second alternative.

Falling to all fours, it sped around Kirk and darted into the forest.

Kirk gazed proudly at the stick in his hands. With a smile he let it drop. He could hear pounding footsteps behind him. His own people.

He held out a hand to the white-furred alien female. "I am Jim Kirk of the *Enterprise*. A friend—a good friend."

She smiled at him. "I am Ola of the world of Lyra. I am most pleased to make the acquaintance of my only husband."

Stepping forward, she threw her long arms around his legs and held him tightly.

Kirk didn't know what to do or say. She had spoken in the universal language. Which was impossible.

Wasn't it?

10

Kirk now had a chance to study the alien female more carefully. Her bare face struck him as very human; in fact, she was almost pretty. Her lips were thin and expressive. Her eyes were round and pink. The top of her head was as hirsute as her body. She had no ears. Her breasts were small, firm, and very feminine. She was young, Kirk guessed, and childless.

"How do you happen to know my language?" he asked her.

"I just speak it, husband," she said glibly.

"No one taught you?"

"I needed no teaching, husband."

Someone behind him guffawed. Kirk turned and glared but couldn't identify the source. Probably one of the security men. "I'm not your husband, Ola," he said.

"But you saved me from the Kova. The others ran away, for they have old wives and hate me. You rescued me."

Kirk knew this wasn't the time to begin learning the local customs. "Ola, I'm not the same as you, am I?"

She shook her head. "You come from outside the world, Captain Kirk."

He had no idea how she knew that. "Among my

49

own people, husbands are different from here. Because I saved you from the Kova does not mean I want you to be my wife."

"But I want to be yours," she said.

"Look, I'm sorry. I . . ."

"No," he said, unwilling to lie. "That's not what I mean. I . . ."

"We can be good friends?"

"Yes, of course." In relief, he gestured behind. "These people can be your friends, too." He introduced Sulu, Uhura, Nurse Chapel, and the two security men to Ola. The security men were Nathan Boggs, a big florid-faced veteran, and Arthur Kaplan, a scrawny young recruit. Everyone bowed to Ola. She bowed back.

"Now, what about your own friends?" Kirk said. "The ones who were with you. Do they come from a settlement? Do you live there?"

She was frowning. "I have no friends. Those were the old ones. They hate me."

"But do you have a home?"

"Yes. In the village of Tumara. I was sent with the old ones to bring you there."

A native village. The sensors hadn't detected that. Or had they? "Are we the only ones who have come to your village lately?"

"Oh, no, there are the other ones," the dark beings who came recently. The Kl . . . Kl . . ."

"Klingons?"

"Yes, them. They took our treasures. He is very angry with them."

Kirk didn't know whom she meant, but he wasn't surprised to discover that the Klingons had been less than perfect guests. Greed and scurrilous behavior were common with them.

"You will follow me to Tumara?" Ola said, pointing into the forest in the direction they had been following.

"We will," said Kirk.

"And you are not my husband?"

He smiled. "No."

"But a friend?"

"A good friend."

"Then I will take you to Domo. Come."

Kirk and the others fell into step behind the alien girl. As they went through the forest, Kirk dropped to the rear of the group. When he was safely out of earshot of Ola, he removed the hand communicator from his belt and flipped open the antenna grid. When Mr. Spock on the bridge of the *Enterprise* answered his call, Kirk quickly described all that had transpired since the party had reached the planetary surface. Spock remained silent, digesting the information, as Kirk spoke. "Well, what do you think?" Kirk said when he finished.

"I find the language question the most puzzling factor, Captain. You said she was quite fluent in the universal language?"

"There wasn't a trace of an accent in her voice. Of course, she might have learned it from Clayton or some other unknown visitor."

"The planet is an extremely large one. Clayton's ship would not have had a sophisticated sensor capability. How could he have found one village on such a huge world?"

"I'm afraid I can't answer that, Mr. Spock."

"Still, it is a possible explanation."

"I agree. On the other hand, there was something else I noticed. Ola seemed to have trouble saying the word 'Klingon.' I got the distinct impression that was because she was accustomed to saying it another way—in their language, not ours."

"You think she may speak Klingonese, too?"

"It's just a guess, Mr. Spock. I'll check into it further and let you know. How about yourself? Anything to report?"

"No, Captain. The situation here remains stable."

"No further calls from the Klingon cruiser?"

"They have remained remarkably silent."

"Good. I'll let you know when we reach the village."

"Fine."

"Kirk out."

Latching the communicator to his belt, Kirk hurried ahead to catch up with the others. Ola turned at his approach and smiled. If she'd noticed his absence, she gave no sign.

11

The trek to the village of Tumara proved to be about as far as Kirk had anticipated: just short of three kilometers overland.

After a kilometer's march through the forest, the trees and bushes fell away, to be replaced by a broad flat meadow filled with tall green grass and bunches of yellow flowers. A gentle steady wind whipped low across the ground, and flocks of flying insects darted ahead of their feet like an escorting army. Kirk wondered what the Klingons thought of this planet. Lyra—Ola had told him that was its name—seemed to him nothing so much as a vast and plentiful garden. How would the endlessly aggressive Klingons ever manage to adapt to such universal tranquillity?

Because of the absence of foliage, the sloping horizon showed more clearly here. Kirk began to understand how a bug must feel trapped at the bottom of an empty bowl. The illusion of severely limited space was difficult to shake. Half-consciously he hunched his shoulders. He stared at the grass directly in front of his feet.

When Ola reached the bank of a narrow twisting river, she turned aside and moved to the left. At last she reached a wooden bridge, and they went

53

over it Kirk realized this was the first true artifact he had seen on this planet. He looked down into the water. A school of fat silver fish went streaking past, easily seen through the clear white water. A garden, he thought once again. Like the mythical Eden, where man had first opened his eyes.

Just past the bridge, the meadow gave way to a squat sloping hill. They climbed to the crest, then went down again. There was another hill, slightly shorter than the first, and they climbed that, too. The village lay huddled in a valley on the opposite side. It wasn't large. From the slope of the hill, Kirk counted fewer than a hundred one-story huts. On closer inspection, he saw that he had overlooked something. The huts were surprisingly well-constructed, making use of what appeared to be steel. There were glass windows and tile roofs. This was advanced technology. But whose?

Ola guided the *Enterprise* party through the narrow streets of Tumara. There were native Lyrans everywhere, but from the amount of interest they showed, the presence of alien visitors might have been an everyday occurrence. The sexes seemed to be equal in numbers, but Kirk noticed the total absence of children. Ola, in fact, was by far the youngest Lyran he had seen. The others were aged, stooped, slow, and balding. Everyone went naked. Tumara was a lazy, languid place. He saw no domestic animals or evidence of agricultural activity. How did the natives feed themselves? he wondered. The forestland was certainly fertile enough to support a village of this size. But was that all? Such a primitive method of subsistence hardly squared with the complexity of the houses themselves. He frowned. Maybe, when their journey ended, they'd find some answers there.

Near the center of the village Ola finally stopped in front of a house that might have been a fraction larger than the others. It also had its own wooden door. On the roof, nearly hidden from sight by the blinding glare of the sun, Kirk noticed a familiar shape. A telescope. He shook his head in wonder. Would the perplexities of this place ever cease?

"You wait here, Jim Kirk," Ola said. "I will bring Domo to greet you." She went forward, knocked on the door to the house, and went inside. A few scattered Lyrans wandered past. None of them even glanced at Kirk and his party.

After a few minutes Ola returned. There was a Lyran male leaning on her arm. He was grotesquely fat, totally bald-headed, and as wrinkled as old parchment. Staring at Kirk from in front of the house, he tried to execute a bow.

"This is Domo," Ola said. "He has come to make you welcome in your new home."

Kirk nodded his head. "I am Captain James Kirk of—"

Domo waved a plump, impatient hand. "Ola has told me your names." He spoke crisply in the universal language. "I will attempt to serve you in any manner possible during your days among those who dwell beneath the constant light."

"I appreciate that very much," Kirk said, though he didn't really understand what Domo was talking about, "but to tell the truth, we aren't here entirely by choice. My ship was captured by some unknown force . . ."

Domo giggled. It was such an unexpected gesture that Kirk stopped and stared. "Isn't it true, James Kirk," said Domo, "that no mere mortal can expect to match wills with something that is greater?"

"Greater? Greater than whom? What are you talking about?"

Domo raised a pudgy finger and pointed to the sky. Kirk looked up, but all he could see was the sun.

"Look, are you the leader of this village—the chief?" Kirk said.

Domo grimaced, showing toothless gums. "I am but one child among many."

"Are you a priest, then?" Kirk thought that might explain a lot of this.

Domo simply looked weary. Leaning over, he whispered softly in Ola's ear.

This is going to be a tough one, Kirk thought. These people may seem innocent, but Domo will be anything but easy to crack.

Kirk was about to interrupt Domo's whisperings when he felt a tug at his sleeve. Turning, he found Uhura standing at his shoulder. She pointed down the street. "Captain, I think we've got company."

Kirk looked where she pointed. A group of Klingons was coming toward them, moving at a rapid clip. The one in the lead—a thin-eyed, dark-bearded officer—held a pistollike weapon in one hand. Suddenly the Klingon raised the weapon. The barrel was pointed at Kirk. The Klingon squeezed his hand shut.

Kirk reached for his belt. So did Uhura, Sulu, and the security men.

They were all too late. The Klingon loosened his grip and grinned broadly.

Kirk knew he ought to be dead—either that or badly stunned.

The Klingon kept coming, his empty hand extended in front of him. "My friend, my friend," he said. "What's wrong? Did I give you a little scare?"

Kirk battled to restrain his temper. He remembered now about his own phaser back in the forest. Was it possible that no weapons worked here on Lyra?

Ignoring the Klingon's proffered hand, he said, "I didn't find that very funny."

The Klingon shrugged. "I was only making a point. On this world, without weapons, we are all equal. There is no reason for us to be anything but friends."

"Who are you?" Kirk said coldly.

"I am Captain Kree of the Imperial Klingon Fleet. These are various members of my crew. You are Kirk, are you not? The famous James T. Kirk?"

"I am." Besides Kree, four other Klingons were present. Three were big, broad-shouldered male officers, but the fourth was a strikingly beautiful young woman. She wore a regulation Klingon uniform of jerkin, shorts, and thigh-length boots, but there was nothing to designate her rank. She met Kirk's curious gaze boldly, her face an expressionless mask. "You don't happen to know what's wrong with our weapons, do you?" Kirk asked Kree.

"You mean old Domo hasn't told you yet?"

"He hasn't told us anything."

"Then I will. Gladly. As a gesture of good fellowship. It's Ay-nab. Ay-nab, the all-powerful. He's the one who deserves credit for imposing the peace."

"Who?" said Kirk. He recognized the name. Ay-nab was the god who haunted Clayton's waking dreams. "When do I get to meet this wondrous being?"

Kree was grinning even more broadly than ever, enjoying his private joke. "But, Captain Kirk, you already have. All of us have. Look. There in the sky. You can see him now."

Kirk looked, as directed, but it was several moments before he realized what Kree meant. Ay-nab was not some abstract spiritual force hiding in an unseen heaven.

Ay-nab was the sun itself.

Here on Lyra, it appeared, the local god was always in the sky.

Kirk turned to ask Domo to confirm what he had guessed. That proved impossible. While Kirk was talking to Kree, Domo had vanished. Ola stood alone in front of the house.

12

The arc of the invisible moon carried it swiftly across the sky, and Kirk found himself walking rapidly, as if to match its unseen pace. The actual moment of eclipse—and night—was still a couple hours away. Nonetheless, Kirk wanted to be sure he was back home well before nightfall.

The village streets, clogged with dozens of Lyrans earlier, were strangely deserted now. Kirk wondered if that, too, had something to do with the near advent of night.

In any event, it made conversation a more private matter. Flicking open his communicator, Kirk called Spock on the *Enterprise* above.

"I'm on my way to the meeting now," Kirk said.

"I won't be able to talk to you again until it's over."

"Are you alone, Captain?"

"That's the way Kree wanted it. I couldn't find a good enough reason to object."

"It could be a trap."

"For what purpose? Even Klingons require motivation."

"Perhaps," Spock said dryly. "Still, you have no further information regarding this meeting?"

"I only know what Kree's message said. He wants to talk to me about making a deal."

"I wonder what you possess that Kree might desire."

"I haven't the vaguest idea. But Kree knows something. He's been here longer than us. He may have the answers to a lot of questions."

"I still don't like it, Captain. I think you should have taken one of the security men along. Kree wouldn't have to know. The man could stay hidden outside."

"Mr. Spock, sometimes you surprise me. That would be cheating, wouldn't it? I never realized how suspicious you could be."

"I do not like Klingons," Spock said with unusual emotion.

"I'm sorry. I never realized the . . . the depth of your feelings."

"Klingons thrive on violence. They seek chaos and create it where it does not exist. They are . . . illogical."

"Well, we'll see," Kirk said with deliberate ambiguity. On the rare occasions when Spock revealed real emotions, Kirk often felt uncomfortable. It was the unexpected nature of the thing, he told himself. "Anything new with Clayton?" he asked, deliberately altering the subject. "Has he said anything else I should know about?"

"Not to my knowledge, Captain. The last time I spoke to Dr. McCoy, Clayton's condition had not improved. Apparently the one period of lucidity he showed was a temporary phenomenon."

"I'd still like to ask him about this god, Ay-nab. Ask McCoy if it's possible to bring Clayton to the bridge where I can talk to him myself. I have a feeling we may have been underestimating Thomas. I think he's a lot saner than we've imagined."

"A sun god can hardly be classified as a rational subject of worship, Captain. One can understand the Lyrans falling into such a primitive form, but Clayton is supposedly a sophisticated man."

"I'd still like to talk with him, Mr. Spock, whether he's a barbarian or not."

"I'll see what I can arrange with Dr. McCoy."

"Thank you, Mr. Spock." Kirk closed the communicator and attached it to his belt. He quickened his pace again. The street was still deserted. He hadn't seen a Lyran since leaving his own house. The sense of isolation disturbed him. He tried to shake off the feeling.

After a brief meeting with Domo in the center of the village, Ola had guided Kirk and his party to three houses. Their new homes, she had said. Kirk placed Sulu and himself in one house, Uhura and Chapel in an adjoining one, and Boggs and Kaplan in the third house, directly across the street. The houses were neat and comfortable, with wooden floors and a few scattered furnishings, largely chairs. Soft furs had been spread upon the floors to serve as beds, and a tanned animal skin hung from each doorway. Because of the infrequency of night upon Lyra, Kirk doubted that cold would ever be much of a problem.

The Klingon message arrived shortly after the party broke up to go to their own homes. An officer delivered it, handing Kirk a slip of paper and immediately disappearing. The message was signed by Captain Kree. It included directions for reaching the house where the Klingons were staying. Kirk never hesitated about going. If Kree could in any way alleviate the ignorance from which he was suffering, Kirk would be more than grateful.

Reaching the house he had been told to seek, Kirk rapped sharply on the wall beside the doorway. The animal skin fluttered back, and a face poked through the gap. It was Kree. "Captain Kirk, my good friend. Do come in."

"Thank you," said Kirk. He entered the house cautiously. Now I know how the fly must have felt when the spider invited him in for dinner, Kirk thought.

The interior of the house was not noticeably different from those Kirk and his party occupied: glass windows, wooden floors, soft furs, a pair of matching chairs.

Kree gestured toward one of the chairs. "Please sit down, Captain. You must be exhausted after your long march here. We followed your progress all the way. It was odd. I had assumed your transporter system was more accurate."

"We didn't want to drop in on you unexpectedly," Kirk said. He glanced at the chair but preferred to keep his feet.

"I hope the young officer I placed in temporary command of my ship did not offend you unnecessarily. I reprimanded him severely when I learned of his attitude toward you. Too often in the past, our species have reacted toward each other with automatic hostility. There is no reason for that here. We can be friends. We're both caught, so to speak, in the same trap."

Kirk shook his head. "I think I may have ended up offending him instead."

Kree chuckled with apparent appreciation. "A silly young pup, yes. Inexperienced. Not sophisticated, in the manner of you and me, not aware of the ways of the cosmos. Are you sure you won't sit?"

Kirk, well aware of the psychological advantage a standing man possessed over one who was sitting, got ready to refuse outright. Just then the animal skin slid back and a third person entered the house.

It was not someone Kirk would have expected. It was the Klingon female. She approached Kree with long, easy strides and spoke in a voice accustomed to command. "Captain, you neglected to inform me that this meeting was in progress."

"My deepest apologies, your highness," Kree said hurriedly. "I wished to brief Captain Kirk before disturbing your rest. Please forgive me." He took her hand deferentially and led her to one of the chairs. When she was safely seated, he turned back to a puzzled Kirk.

"I don't believe you two have been properly in-
troduced," he said. "Captain Kirk, I want you to meet
Princess Kyanna, legitimate heir to the throne of the
Klingon Empire."

13

When Princess Kyanna pointed to the chair beside her own, Kirk thought it was finally time to sit. Captain Kree, smiling broadly, hovered above them. "The Princess has an offer to make," he said, by way of introduction.

"I assume you've explained our situation to Captain Kirk," she said.

"Ah, no," Kree said. "I'm afraid I didn't—"

"Then I will." She swiveled in her chair, facing Kirk. A striking woman, he thought. Like a female snake. "Captain Kree and I are outlaws. My uncle, the present illegitimate Emperor, has sentenced us both to die under trumped-up charges of treason. Necessity caused the Captain and me to join forces. The crew of any Klingon warship is loyal first to their commander and then to the Empire. Because of that, Captain Kree offered me the use of his battlecruiser."

Kirk tried to look politely interested. Internal Klingon politics were much too complex for anyone but a scholar to follow. Assassination, rebellion, and civil war were common occurrences among them. Most Federation statesmen regarded this instability as a blessing. As long as the Klingons kept busy warring upon each other, the other races of the Galaxy were that much safer.

"I mention these details," Princess Kyanna went on, "only because I want you to realize how I came to be here. I am not unlearned in astronomical matters. It was my opinion that the multitude of stars found here at the Core would provide cover to evade my pursuers until such time as my supporters at home might rally a cause. Unfortunately, when our ship passed this strange world, a force took hold of our engines and brought us here. For some time we remained in orbit around the central sun. Then a message came, instructing us to land here. We transported down and found this village."

"A message? Who sent it?"

"We have no idea. It was . . . telepathic. A voice spoke in my mind. We asked the natives' priest, this creature Domo. He said it was Ay-nab."

"The sun god," said Kirk.

"So they claim. But we believe . . ." Suddenly she yawned. "Captain Kree, I grow weary. Perhaps you could explain to Captain Kirk about these peculiar local beliefs." Turning away from Kirk, she crossed her long legs at the knee. Her high leather boots made a crinkling noise as they touched.

"The Lyrans," Kree said, "are fully aware that they live on a solitary world moving through space. They believe that this is the work of Ay-nab and that he is, in fact, carrying them across the Galaxy to a particular destiny. They believe that in time their planet will rendezvous with a mysterious dark place that will destroy their world and them with it. They believe—"

"I don't believe any of this is relevant, Captain." Princess Kyanna was glaring. Kirk sensed that Captain Kree might have said more than he should. "Please explain what our theories are."

Looking more amused than chastised, Kree went on. "The point is, Captain Kirk, that the Lyrans have no intention of letting us leave this world until we are dead. They seem to think we've been brought here to share their destiny. Since it's the will of their god, there's nothing they can do. We Klingons, as you may know, long ago rejected any possibility that a supreme being might exist."

"Then you think the natives themselves are capable of letting us go."

Kree shook his head, dismissing the thought instantly. "Naturally not. The Lyrans are hardly more than animals who talk. But something's keeping us here. Something took control of both our ships. Something spoke telepathically to the Princess."

"Yes, but what?" said Kirk.

Princess Kyama came suddenly alert. Shifting in her chair, she smiled at Kirk. It was a gorgeous smile, broad and open. And undoubtedly extremely rare, he thought. "That's where we need your help, Captain. You see, this village can't be all. Somewhere on this planet there must exist a highly advanced race of some kind. Our cruiser is a warship, designed for deep-space combat. You possess certain resources we lack, resources that might permit you to detect and contact this other race."

Her observation was meant at least partially as a question. Kirk told the truth. "We have found nothing of the kind." He didn't add that he was quite convinced that no such advanced race existed on Lyra.

"But if you did, with your sensors and your computer, devices which we, candidly, lack, you would not keep this information secret."

"Of course not, Princess."

She frowned, plainly skeptical of his sincerity. "When I invited you here, I mentioned the possibility of striking a deal. I want you to know that I'm not unwilling to offer something in return for your assistance, Captain Kree, please explain."

"The Princess refers to a store of advanced weaponry we happened to discover hidden here in the village," Kree said. "These weapons are extremely powerful—additional evidence, we believe, of the existence of a superior race on this world—and we hope to carry some of them away whenever we finally leave this damnable planet. The Princess has authorized me to offer you a share of these weapons in return for your assistance in obtaining our mutual release."

"And these weapons work?"

"Oh, yes. Quite adequately. In fact, if you doubt my testimony, I can arrange a brief display."

"I think I'd like that."

Princess Kyanna, sensing Kirk's hesitation, intervened. "Of course, our only purpose in obtaining these weapons is to use them against my uncle, the usurping Emperor. We have no aggressive designs of our own."

"Of course not," said Kirk.

"I can arrange the display for you within the hour," Kree said.

Kirk shook his head. He was beginning to get restless. This meeting had dragged on far longer than he had anticipated. The strain of constantly trying to ferret out the truth behind the Klingons' veil of constant falsehoods was wearing on him. "I believe it's going to get dark around here in less time than that."

Both Kree and the Princess looked very disturbed. "I'm afraid we weren't aware of that," she said.

"But a few hours can't make much of a difference," Kirk said. "I'll be glad to see these weapons, once daylight returns."

Princess Kyanna appeared less than satisfied. "But you won't make us wait, will you? Your sensors can continue to seek out the location of this advanced race. You won't keep anything from us?"

"If we find anything, I'll tell you." Kirk stood up. He nodded to Kree, then bowed to Princess Kyanna.

"And, Captain . . . ?" she said.

Kirk paused halfway to the door. "Yes, Princess?"

"I wanted to warn you. These natives may look peaceful, but at night strange things can happen. If I were you, I'd remain indoors until morning. It's a wise course. We always follow it."

"I appreciate your advice, Princess." Kirk went on outside.

It already seemed noticeably cooler. The sky had assumed a grayish tint. Kirk knew it might be only his imagination. The sun was a full disk in the center of the sky. He moved through the empty streets at a hurried pace. Whatever the case at the moment, darkness—the eclipse—could not be far away.

Opening the communicator, he called Spock and quickly summarized the details of the meeting with Kree and Princess Kyanna. "And there is one thing I want you to do for me, Mr. Spock. Have Chekov project a course based on this planet's present velocity and direction. I want to know where we're headed. Princess Kyanna was awfully eager to get away from here. I want to see if we can find out why."

"Surely you place no credence in this myth of a dark place where the planet will be destroyed."

"At the moment, Mr. Spock, I'm keeping an open mind. Most myths have some basis in fact. Maybe this one does, too."

"I'll speak to Mr. Chekov at once."

"Thank you, Mr. Spock."

As he closed the communicator and prepared to cover the final few meters home, Kirk turned his eyes to the sky once more. The edge of the sun had vanished as thoroughly as if it had been sliced away by a huge razor. Seeing this, Kirk suppressed a cold shiver. It was a primitive response to the coming of night. As he moved through the empty streets, past the silent darkening houses, he felt sure he wasn't alone in feeling this way.

As Kirk put out a hand and pushed aside the animal skin hanging from the doorway, he heard high, tinkling laughter coming from inside. Whoever that was, it wasn't Sulu, he decided, stepping inside.

Ola, the young Lyran girl, sat cross-legged on the floor. Crouched beside her, Lieutenant Sulu clutched a playing card in one hand. He made quick circling motions through the air. "Now, watch closely," he said. "Don't let your eyes lose sight of the card. Watch closely . . . closely . . . closely . . ."

Holding her breath, Ola followed the path of the card. Kirk caught a flash of color. A face card. Either a king or a jack, he decided.

Suddenly, with a snap, Sulu turned his wrist. "Presto!" he cried.

The card had vanished.

Releasing her breath in an excited burst, Ola laughed uproariously, eyes wide with astonishment. "You made it disappear. It is like magic."

"You bet," Sulu said. He showed her the palms of his hands, then the backs. "See? Nothing up my sleeve. Gone. Absolutely gone. Now, where do you think it went?"

"It is gone," she said.

Sulu nodded solemnly. "But where?"

"Where?"

68

"Give it a guess," Glancing up, Sulu spotted Kirk for the first time. He grimaced sheepishly. "Oh, hello, Captain. I was just teaching Ola how—"

"Please proceed, Mr. Sulu," Kirk folded his arms across his chest and leaned in the doorway. "I'm interested to see how this comes out myself."

"Yes, Sulu," said Ola, bouncing on the floor. "Where is that card, please?"

Encouraged, Sulu shut his eyes. "I'm trying to see it now. Trying to focus. Trying to see. Trying . . . trying . . ." His forehead wrinkled with the exertion of the search. "It is . . . it is . . . it is—*here.*"

Reaching quickly out, he slipped a hand behind Ola's head and an instant later gripped the missing card in his fingers. "Why, here it is now."

Ola threatened to explode with laughter.

Grinning in spite of himself, Kirk pushed away from the wall. "Now, that's a talent of yours I didn't know about, Mr. Sulu. Your personnel records never gave a hint."

Sulu tried his best not to look embarrassed. "It's just something I've picked up, Captain. A way of entertaining the crew. I'm not really proficient yet."

"Well, lucky for the rest of us," Kirk said. "If you were, no telling what you might make disappear. Me, for instance."

"Never you, Captain Kirk."

"Well, then perhaps just Mr. Spock. I understand he's regarded as an even harsher slavemaster than I." Kirk bent low, looking at Ola. Nestled on the floor, she seemed as delicate as a doll. "And how are you? Did you enjoy Mr. Sulu's trick?"

"Oh, it was masterful, Captain Kirk. Truly magical." Her eyes glowed like a child's on Christmas. How much could she possibly know of this strange world?

"And did you come here for a reason?"

"I . . ." She seemed to lose her confidence all at once. "I wanted to know if you had changed your mind about being my husband."

Kirk looked at Sulu, who immediately averted his eyes. "No, Ola, I'm afraid not," he said softly.

"That is too bad. When you saved me from the Kova, I thought . . ."

Kirk felt less than comfortable, but he knew this was something that should be faced. The girl, Ola, deserved that much. "Isn't there someone here in the village, someone of your own race, whom you could marry?"

"They are all old. If I am to marry at all, it must be a stranger."

"You mean everyone's old? Aren't there any children?"

"I was the last born. Since me, there have been no others, and now everyone is old. Domo says it is Ay-nab's wish. Soon we will reach the dark place where we will die. I wanted to have a husband before I died."

"I'm sorry to disappoint you, Ola." Kirk started to move around the room. What she'd told him was both puzzling and disturbing. Could it be true? He doubted that Ola would lie, and he certainly hadn't seen anyone obviously younger than she. The opposite, actually. Everyone else did seem old.

"Ola, can you tell me something? The Klingons. You know them. Didn't you mention having some trouble with them?"

"Only that they took our treasures," she said. "What are these treasures?"

"Oh, terrible things. Machines that kill and destroy. Domo told me about them. He said Ay-nab wished the treasures to remain hidden forever, but the Klingons learned of their existence and removed them from the ground. It was a very bad thing to do, but Ay-nab will take them in time, and then the treasures will be returned to the ground."

"What will Ay-nab do?"

"Consume them, claim them." She looked at the

floor, as if hesitant to speak. "It is the way of Ay-nab to claim all strangers as his own."

"Even us?" asked Kirk.

She nodded slowly. "Even you." She seemed sad. "It has always been the way. I should not talk of it to you, but there is nothing anyone can do to thwart the will of the god."

"Do you mean that others have come to Lyra before us and the Klingons?"

"Oh, yes, many others. Some I have seen, most I have not, for I am very young. Domo could tell you more, but he is forbidden to speak."

"Did you ever know a man named Thomas Clayton?"

"I . . . yes, I knew him. He is a Stranger now. I . . ." She stopped, as if just becoming aware of her surroundings. Her eyes were wide. Kirk looked around and realized what must be wrong. It was growing dark. Night had come to Lyra.

Ola sprang to her feet. "I must go. The Strangers will be—"

Kirk grabbed her arm and held her. "Ola, what's wrong?"

"The blackness." She twisted in his grip. "They will come from the resting place to . . . to . . ." She looked fearfully at the doorway, then back to Kirk.

He decided to let her go. "Would you like me to go home with you?"

"No!" She was nearly screaming. "You must stay here. It is much worse for you than me."

"Then why don't you stay here? If you're afraid, you can leave when it's light again."

She gazed at him in open wonder. "You are such a good person, Captain Kirk. Yes, I will stay. It is better for all of us that way."

"Good." Kirk turned around. "Mr. Sulu, you'd better light a torch. In a few more minutes we won't be able to see our own hands."

Sulu searched through their gear. In a moment a

bright light flared in his hand. Kirk heard a sharp cry and turned. It was Ola. She stood with her arms dangling loosely at her sides, her face a mask of wonderment. She was staring at the bright yellow light.

Not even fire? Kirk thought. Didn't they even know about that?

15

Captain's Log, Stardate 6533.9:

This is being recorded by Science Officer Spock, temporarily in command of the ship.

Contact with Captain Kirk and his landing party continues at frequent intervals. At the present, it is nighttime in the village of Tumara, a temporary phenomenon caused by an eclipse of the sun by one of the planet's twelve apparently artificial satellites. It is my intention, once this has passed, to speak again with Captain Kirk. In the meantime, I have ordered the crew to assume a light-duty status. Primary among my own endeavors has been an attempt to obtain a computer projection capable of solving the major paradoxes of this planet. Unfortunately, my results have been more disturbing than illuminating. The computer stubbornly insists that any total solution must be predicated upon the assumption that the internal sun of Lyra is a conscious and powerful deity. It is my hope that additional input will force an alteration in this projection.

"No crisp, logical answers, Mr. Spock?" said a soft, drawling voice from behind. Turning away from the library/computer console, Spock discovered Dr. Leonard McCoy lurking near his elbow. Spock shook his head and switched off the console.

"I'm afraid, Doctor, that the answers I am receiving tend more to the magical than the logical. The computer insists this sun must be a conscious entity."

"A computer that believes in God. Well, what do you know?"

Spock shook his head. "Not necessarily a god, Doctor. Such beings probably do not exist. Advanced intelligences, however, most certainly do."

"Not in the middle of suns. If they did, they'd need to wear some pretty tough asbestos suits."

"The theory of such intelligences has been broached speculatively in the past."

"Don't tell me you're starting to believe in God, too."

"It's possible, Doctor, though hardly probable. The evolution of such an intelligence would be difficult to determine. Still, there is no irrefutable reason why such a being cannot exist."

"Well, if you ever find one, be sure to let me know, Spock. I've got a lot of praying to catch up on each night before I go to bed."

"I'm sure a logical god would comprehend the basis for your fallen state, Doctor. Didn't Christ say 'Father, forgive them, for they know not what they do'?"

"And just what do you mean by that crack?" McCoy said, bristling.

Spock shook his head apologetically. "Why nothing, Doctor, nothing at all." Inwardly he grinned. Whether McCoy knew it or not, he had just been twitted. It was a sport Spock enjoyed practicing every now and then. The paradox with Dr. McCoy was that, for a generally illogical being, he was at times also amazingly literal.

Apparently satisfied by Spock's apology, McCoy crossed the nearly empty bridge, Ensign Chekov sat alone, absorbed in a thick stack of computer printouts. McCoy spun Sulu's empty chair around and sat down. "This is getting to be a damned bore," he told Spock. "Do you know that not one person appeared for sick call this morning? And do you know why? It's the light-duty status you've ordered. Everyone is so busy having fun, they can't take a few moments to get sick."

"I would have thought that a healthy crew would be a source of pride for you."

"Pride, sure, but what's that got to do with being bored? I wish Jim would let me beam down to that Garden of Eden of his. It ought to be a fascinating world. How about you, Spock? How'd you like to stand with your big feet on the ground and see the horizon soaring up away from you like the sides of a big cup?"

"It would be a most interesting illusion, to be sure."

"An interesting illusion? That's all?"

"Should there be more?"

McCoy shook his head wearily. "For you, maybe that's enough. For me, it never can be. What's the use of the extraordinary, the unique, if such things fail to move us in extraordinary and unique ways?"

"Perhaps there is no use," Spock said.

"That's an awfully bleak philosophy."

"Logic is never bleak, Doctor. Only truthful."

"Factual, you mean. It takes imagination, romance, and poetry to reflect the whole of the truth."

These arguments between Spock and McCoy had been raging for as long as the two had known each other. Nothing was ever settled; neither ever won a clear victory. Both enjoyed the combat thoroughly as an end in itself.

"What's the present condition of Thomas Clayton?" Spock asked. He felt the time was right for a strategic change in subject matter. "When I talk to Captain Kirk again, I'll have to tell him what's occurred."

"I know." McCoy shook his head. "On my way up here, I stopped by his cell, but there's been no change. He's totally comatose. According to the medic I put in the room, Clayton hasn't moved a muscle in more than an hour. I don't like it, Spock. There was no reason for his condition to worsen."

"You had no warning?"

"None at all. In fact, I thought he was getting better again."

"Then you should hardly blame yourself, Doctor."

"I appreciate your saying that, Spock."

"It's only the truth, Doctor. Only logic."

Seemingly unaware of anyone or anything else, Ensign Chekov continued to study the computer data stacked on his console. Chekov was performing the calculations Captain Kirk had requested, projecting a future course for the planet Lyra. Spock had not asked for a preliminary report, and Chekov, who knew from experience that Spock preferred to receive facts only in finished form, had kept silent about any tentative discoveries he might have made.

McCoy leaned back in his chair and locked his hands around one knee. "Spock, since we're both stuck here with not enough to do, maybe there's one thing we ought to settle once and for all. I've got a riddle for you, and I'm willing to wager . . . oh, say, a bottle of good bourbon that you can't come up with an answer. The riddle is a problem in logic. At least, on the surface that's what it is. I'm betting that logic has its limits as a means of solving problems. How about it? Willing to put a bottle of whiskey where your mouth is?"

Coming closer, Spock leaned over and sniffed McCoy's breath. "I had to be sure you hadn't been drinking," he explained. "My ethical code forbids me to take advantage of an intoxicated mind."

McCoy frowned. "No, dammit, I haven't touched a drop, but I will, after I've won this bet, with you paying. Now, how about it, Spock? Are you in this or not?"

"Of course I am, Doctor."

"Good. Now, listen closely. Here's the riddle. Once there was an island. A desert island, with ocean all around. Two people lived on this island: a father and his son. They were stranded. The father was very old. He had a white beard that reached to his navel, and skin as wrinkled as an elephant's. Know what an elephant is, Mr. Spock?"

"My studies of extinct Earth species have been quite extensive."

"Good. Because I wouldn't want to be accused of taking advantage of your ignorance. Now, the boy was young, barely out of puberty. He was weak and sickly and not very intelligent. The father, despite his age, knew how to survive on the island and keep both of them alive. The boy didn't.

"And the mother?" said Spock.

"What?"

"From what you've said, I assume the boy must have been born on the island. You haven't explained the absence of a mother."

McCoy glared. "Don't ask me silly questions, Spock. She drowned. Sharks ate her up. How should I know what happened to the mother?"

"I'm sorry. I didn't mean to disturb you. Please go on, Doctor. I'll endeavor to ignore the missing mother."

"Thank you, Mr. Spock. Now, one day there was a severe earthquake on the island. The quake opened up the earth and exposed a long-buried cave. Up out of this cave came a huge monster. It was twenty meters long, with scaly green skin, a spiked tail, forked tongue, and fiery breath. The monster loomed over the father and son and told them it was hungry."

Spock shook his head. "My studies in Earth zoology failed to make note of such a talking monster."

"It was a rare mutation," McCoy said. "The monster explained that it was going to have to eat someone. Only one, because it wasn't greedy, and the other could survive. The monster asked which of them wanted to eaten. The father said it was a difficult matter to decide. He asked the monster for ten minutes in which to make up his mind. The monster granted this request. Now, the two of them lived in a small hut, and—"

"I thought you said it was a desert island," Spock said.

McCoy looked up. "Yes, I did. So what?"

"How can a hut exist in a desert?"

McCoy looked irritated. "It wasn't all desert. There were a few trees. Palm trees."

"Then this hut was constructed from wood?"

"If that's the way you want it, yes. Let me finish my story, Spock."

"I only sought clarification on that one specific point. Please proceed, Doctor."

"Thank you again, Mr. Spock." McCoy took a deep breath, then went on. "The monster told the old man he would go away for ten minutes, but when he returned, he expected to find one of them waiting for him in front of the hut. Alone, the father and son discussed the matter. Eventually they reached a decision. In ten minutes the monster returned. What did he find in front of the hut? Who was there?"

Spock frowned. "That's the riddle?"

"That's it," McCoy said, nodding firmly. "What's wrong? Trouble, Mr. Spock? You know why? Because it's a problem of the heart, not the mind, and even though you have a heart—your medical records say you do—you've never learned to listen to it and act accordingly. Give up?"

Spock shook his head, eyes closed in concentration.

"Give me a moment, please."

"Why? What's the problem?"

"I need to consider all the possibilities."

"What possibilities? There can be only two. The father is old. No matter what, he'll die soon. The son, however, is unable to survive on his own. So which should it be, Mr. Spock? The father or the son? Come on. Let's hear a solution."

"A solution?" Spock opened his eyes. "Oh, that's obvious enough," he said matter-of-factly. "The monster will of course find nothing."

"Nothing?" said McCoy, coming halfway out of his chair.

"Logically, yes. Since the monster was foolish enough to go away, the men will have used that time to take apart their wooden hut. With the logs, they will then construct a raft. I assume the monster cannot swim. Because of its shape and bulk, I would strongly disagree if you attempted to claim that it could. The men will push their raft into the ocean and hop aboard. The monster is hungry. In time, it will starve. If the men bring sufficient supplies onto the raft and supplement these with fish from the sea, they can easily wait him out. Once the monster has died, the men can safely return home and reconstruct their hut."

"Spock, Spock, Spock," McCoy said. "I can't believe you could—"

"I'm only offering a logical solution, Doctor."

Before McCoy's temper could explode, a voice said, "Please put your hands in the air."

Spock spun around. A thin man dressed in a medic's uniform stood beside the turbolift. Spock realized in an instant who it must be: Thomas Clayton.

Clayton held a hand phaser in his fingers.

"Clayton, you damned fool," McCoy said, springing to his feet. "What are you—?"

"Easy, Doctor." Clayton waved the phaser. "I hurt you once. Don't make me do it again."

Spock gripped McCoy's sleeve. "Remember, this man is not rational."

"He's also supposed to be comatose. Clayton, what did you do to the medic in your room?"

"I merely borrowed his uniform and phaser. He's unharmed."

"What do you want here?" Spock said.

"I want you. I want . . ." Clayton broke off with a

sharp laugh. "Me? I want nothing. It is Ay-nab. He has ordered me to return to his world. You and Dr. McCoy will come, too. It is time for all of us to gaze upon the shining eye of the god."

16

As far as Spock could see, the village of Tumara closely resembled Captain Kirk's description of it, and yet in the dark it also seemed to be a mysterious and ominous place, with empty streets, dark houses, and a constant chilling wind.

"Do you have a particular destination in mind?" Spock asked. The faint figure of Thomas Clayton, phaser in hand, loomed behind him. They stood somewhere near the outskirts of the village.

"Just start walking," Clayton said. "When it's time to turn or stop, I'll tell you."

"You won't get away with this, you know," Dr. McCoy said. "I really don't know what you expect to gain."

"Just walk, please."

With an angry grunt McCoy stepped forward. Spock moved beside him. Above, only the scarlet corona of the sun spilling around the disk of the dark moon provided any light to guide them. Lyra was a world without stars. Still, the ground was smooth and flat. The hulking outlines of the houses stood out clearly.

Behind them, Clayton started laughing. It was a private sound, intended only for himself.

"Thomas, why don't you put down the phaser?"

McCoy said. "We're here now, Spock and I won't bother you."

Clayton's laughter went on. He muttered something, but his words vanished in the wind.

"We don't want an accident," McCoy said.

"An accident?" Clayton cried with sudden shrillness. "There are no accidents under the eye of a god."

Spock was remembering what Captain Kirk had told him, how neither his own hand weapons nor those of the Klingons had functioned here. In a logical universe, that observation would have strongly indicated that Clayton's weapon would not work either. But could he trust logic here? There was a presence, almost a voice. Spock sensed that something was very wrong here, and it disturbed him deeply.

Spock slowed his pace. Suddenly he stopped. Clayton, walking close behind, bumped into him. McCoy turned and looked back. "What is it, Spock?"

"I'm not sure." Spock took a tentative step. Then he heard it—again. Footsteps. Nearby.

"Hey, move it," Clayton said. He gave Spock a shove.

"Sorry." Spock moved forward. "I tripped over a rock."

Spock caught up with McCoy. The footsteps came with him. He heard them clearly now, off to the left, parallel with a line of houses.

"What was that about?" McCoy whispered. Clayton laughing again, could not hear them.

"I'm not sure."

"Did you see something?"

"No, not that."

Not seen—heard. Who could it be? he wondered. The Lyrans, according to Captain Kirk, were a small, fragile race. These footsteps were as heavy as a man's. It wouldn't likely be Kirk or his group. They would have intervened by now.

"You weren't trying to make a break for it? It's so dark. We might have a shot at it."

"I don't think so." Spock did not regard the situation as sufficiently critical to justify the risk of lives. "I'm curious to discover what Clayton intends."

"If anything. The man's not stable."

"He hasn't harmed anyone so far."

"That phaser of his may not work down here. Do you remember what Jim said?"

Spock wasn't surprised that McCoy also remembered.

"I remember. But it may work."

"I can wait, if you can."

"I think it's wiser." Spock was listening to the footsteps. They had moved ahead now, as if anticipating the route Clayton would follow.

"Turn left," Clayton said.

Compliantly, Spock and McCoy turned left. The footsteps turned, too. Spock thought there might be more than one set. He glanced at the sky. The sun seemed to be edging out from behind the moon. There was additional light. He squinted into the darkness.

They turned twice more. Right, then left, then a third turn, right again. Down the street, Spock spied a distant glow. He knew without asking that this was where they were headed. It was the one evidence of life he had seen since reaching this world.

The sky was brighter now. The footsteps were farther ahead. The man—or men, or whatever—remained just out of sight.

Touching McCoy's sleeve, Spock leaned close and whispered, "I think I should inform you. Someone has been following us for some time. They're ahead now. Keep a watchful eye. We're drawing close, and something may happen."

"A Lyran?"

"I don't think so. I . . ." Spock strained at the darkness. The gleam of light ahead had separated into three distinct squares. Three windows—three houses. It must be Kirk and the others.

"Then who could it be?"

"I wish I could . . ." Then all at once Spock saw clearly. A standing figure, as tall as any man, stood rooted in the path ahead. McCoy let out a shout of surprise.

Clayton saw the figure at the same time. He made a strangled cry and swung his phaser up. Simultaneously, the man charged forward. Caught in between, Spock threw himself to one side. His shoulder bumped McCoy and sent him sprawling. A phaser hummed. Spock sensed the bolt flashing overhead. He hugged the ground. "Bastards!" screamed Clayton. "I got away! I won't come back! I won't!" Spock heard dwindling footsteps. The phaser hummed again. There was a cry, and something hit the ground hard. Spock heard laughter. Another phaser bolt tore through the air. "Bastards!" said Clayton. "Dirty, dead, foul . . ."

Spock sensed that the time had come. Springing to his feet, he swung his hand. His fingers pinched the soft flesh of a shoulder.

Thomas Clayton crumpled in the dust.

Spock wheeled around. There was no one else to be seen.

Picking himself up, McCoy brushed the dust off his trousers. "What the hell is going on?"

"Get his phaser." Spock pointed to where Clayton lay. "I'll check the other one."

"What other . . . ?"

There was a second body lying in the dust. Crouching, Spock gently rolled the man over on his back. He put his ear against the heart and listened attentively. At first he seemed to hear nothing; then all at once the heart beat strongly.

"How is he?" McCoy hovered over him, holding Clayton's phaser. "And who is he?"

"I don't know. He's alive. Check the phaser."

McCoy glanced at the weapon. "It's set to kill," he said slowly.

"Well, he's not dead. Maybe you ought to take a look."

McCoy bent down. The man's face was old and thin, like a skull. "He's not one of us, that's for sure."

The man wore the blue shirt and black flared trousers of a Star Fleet science officer. The insignia on his chest, five interlocking circles, was not that of the *Enterprise.*

"I've never seen that patch before," McCoy said.

"It's not current."

"Not current? Not the *Rickover?*" McCoy looked up with wide eyes.

Spock nodded thoughtfully. "The *Rickover,*" he confirmed.

17

Even though outside darkness held firm sway, it did not seem noticeably cooler in here. Not warm, but rather comfortable. Almost perfect. Still, Lieutenant Uhura could not fall asleep.

She lay snuggled between soft furs on the hard floor of the house she shared with Christine Chapel. Stretching, yawning, twisting, tossing from side to side, she heard the gentle murmur of Chapel's sleeping breath from nearby. For Uhura the problem lay in the tension that still remained from a long and exciting day. She couldn't risk a sleeping potion. Night was brief on Lyra, and too soon she would need to be awake and alert. The events of the past day filled her mind like holograms in a newstape. The search for life on Lyra. Beaming down. The trek through the shimmering forest. The strange apparition of Ola. Kirk's battle with the Kova. The march into the village. Domo. Klingons. She knew she ought to sleep. Captain Kirk would want it. She was tired. Too tired to stand. Too tired, perhaps, to sleep.

Rolling on her back, Uhura fixed the fur so that it barely covered her breasts. She wiggled her toes, stretched her knees, put her hands behind her head, and strained to see the ceiling in the dark. Now, what was a good method? A foolproof means for inducing sleep to visit the sleepless? She knew a variety of techniques. The trouble was, in her present state of mind she found it impossible to concentrate for long on any one of them.

Kirk and Sulu, she knew, had chosen to remain awake and wait out the dawn. The light from their house spilled through the window above her head. Across the street, Boggs and Kaplan were also awake. She could see their light, though faintly, through another window. She was a scientist. Scientists needed their wits at all times. She'd made a phrase once. What was it? *The most common characteristic of any scientist is his (or her) total inability to get along with any other scientist.* She blamed specialization. Every scientist knew one subject so intimately that everything else in the cosmos assumed a shadowy, insubstantial, phantasmagoric form. For a good physicist, biology was an arcane discipline; for a biologist, physics was obscure.

The *Enterprise* was fortunate to have Mr. Spock. He, she often believed, was the one thing that prevented the ship's scientific complement from disintegrating totally. Spock was no specialist. Spock was an anachronism, like Leonardo, in the way that he often seemed to know everything about everything. Music, for example. Uhura loved music with deep passion. She collected songs the way some people collected old books or coins. Yet Spock knew more. He couldn't sing—or wouldn't—but he could tell her better than anyone else when her own voice went wrong. Spock wasn't an artist. He never claimed to create. Spock knew. He was a scholar in the very best sense of that word.

Christine Chapel in her sleep suddenly groaned and let loose a ripple of laughter.

Well, thought Uhura, turning on her right side, now, wasn't that odd? Here she was thinking about Mr. Spock, while beside her slept poor Chapel, who was in love with him, very possibly dreaming of the same man. Spock did not love Chapel. Could he ever fall in love? She vividly remembered when Captain Kirk, disobeying orders, had taken Spock to Vulcan, where he was scheduled to marry a female he had known as a child. Something had gone terribly wrong on Vulcan—she never learned exactly what—and Spock had returned alone and resumed his old duties. Still, that had never been love, not as she understood the term; it was a biological urge. If Spock did not mate, he would die.

What of herself? As deeply as she admired Mr. Spock, she did not love him in any truly emotional sense. She was not Chapel, content to love without return. In fact, she did not think she loved anyone, a lack that sometimes affected her with pain. She had never loved anyone. And yet, when she sang of love—and many of her songs (even the ones Spock had taught her) dealt with that subject—she knew perfectly well what the composers had intended when they'd first spun their complex webs of words and sounds. If she wasn't in love and never had been, it was not because of the smallness of her heart but rather because (to use an old cliché) the right man had never come along. When would he? Ever? She had no way of knowing. Despite the diligent efforts of thousands of men and women—scientists, sorcerers, mathematicians, magicians—the future remained a dark and unseeable realm.

If duty had not interfered, she might have fallen in love with Kirk. Since the day she had first stepped on board the *Enterprise*, she had been aware of how she could feel for him. "Welcome aboard, Ensign," he'd said. (She remembered this first conversation as clearly today as when it had occurred.) "Thank you, sir." "Uhura—don't I know that name?" "In Swahili it means 'truth.'" "Do you have an older brother?" "I think you may mean my father." "A starman?" "He was." "One of the best." "And one of the last—he's dead now." "Oh, I'm sorry to hear that.

He was quite a man." "He disappeared in space two years ago." "That's unfortunate."

Odd that they had talked about her father. He and Captain Kirk were much alike. Her father had been a starman, the term given to those few humans who had initiated the exploration of the Galaxy long before the establishment of Star Fleet with its huge ships and giant crews. Lone men and women who had visited unexplored worlds and performed the same tasks now handled by as many as four hundred. Her father was almost the last of his kind. A man living out of time. As a child, she had seen him only occasionally. His domain was space, not Earth. She had grown up in Dakar, one of the twin capitals of the United States of Africa. A beautiful city, bathed in the glow of the blue Atlantic. An African city, a cosmopolitan city, but one still very much the product of its French colonial heritage. During the nineteenth century, Dakar had been one of four Senegalese towns holding a privileged place in the French Empire. Eventually the residents were even granted full French citizenship and allowed to choose their own representatives to sit in the Chamber of Deputies in Paris. The French attempted to institute a colonial policy of assimilation, and while that failed miserably—few Africans wished to be made over into dark-skinned Frenchmen—the French influence left its mark not only upon the city of Dakar but also upon those, like Uhura, who were born generations after the colonists departed. She spoke French as fluently—and naturally—as Swahili. Her favorite songs were French. Her favorite foods. The greatest writer who ever lived, she believed, was the French novelist Marcel Proust. The greatest painters, the French Impressionists. Her father had developed and shared most of these preferences. That was how she best remembered him, his unexpected visits home, when he would take her and her mother to Paris for several glorious weeks before eventually returning—always too soon—to the realm he loved best. When word reached her of his death, she had not seen him for three years. The last time was in Paris. She was seventeen.

All at once she noticed a sound in the room, a peculiar tapping noise. Half-consciously she sat up, pushed back the fur, and stood, naked except for a filmy underskirt. For a moment she listened intently, but the sound, whatever it had been, did not recur. Still, she was certain it had come from outside. On tiptoes she crossed to the window facing the street. She peered through the glass.

There was a face, staring back.

She caught her breath and looked again: she knew this face, knew this man.

As if in a dream, she pedaled away from the window and, turning, went to the door. She opened it softly and went outside.

The bite of a cold wind struck her bare flesh. Hugging herself, shivering, she moved stiffly. Above, the sun's flaming corona peeped past the dark disk of the moon. She limped on bare feet. The taste of dust was strong on her lips and tongue. Odd, she thought, the multitude of sensations. Most often, in a dream, verisimilitude was a thin fabric floating upon a fog of unreality. Only a few key details rang true; the rest remained obscure. But this was a dream. It had to be. There was no one in front of the house. She stepped around to the side. A light shone in Kirk's window. She heard voices, laughter. Ducking low, she crept past, not wanting to disturb them. She felt uncomfortable, undressed as she was. Aboard ship, people practiced modesty purely for disciplinary reasons. This wasn't the ship. It was just a dream. How could it matter what anyone saw? She passed another corner. And stopped. "Who are you?" she asked the dark figure. "I know you."

Fingers stroked her face—stiff, cold fingers, like the dead. She stood rigidly.

"Father?" she said. "Father, it is you."

She could not see him clearly. His features were insubstantial, not firmly set. His hands touched her cheeks, cradled her chin. He was a giant of a man. Tilting her head, she strained to see his eyes.

Yes, he had changed. Older—oh, incredibly older—his face as thin as a skull, eyes hollow. The hair on his head was as white as a ghost. Yes, she thought quickly, that's what he is: a ghost. The living reflection of a dead man. But was he dead? The hands on her face, though cold, tingled with the essence of life.

"Father, you can't know how much I've missed you. I . . ." Her head drooped against his chest. She cried silently. Strong, powerful arms embraced her shoulders.

"You are cold," he said. She knew his voice.

"I came . . . when I heard you. There wasn't time to dress."

"I understand." He chuckled consolingly, a deep bass sound echoing in the cavity of his chest. The familiar laugh cut through her like a knife. "You must go back. I'll wait. This is a cold and terrible place, daughter."

"I . . . I hate it."

"I'm with you now."

"I know."

"Then come with me." He took her hand. They went the opposite way, where Kirk could not see them. At the door, his cold lips brushed hers. "Remember that I love you and always have."

"I know."

"You've doubted."

"No, never."

"Even when I stayed away so much?"

"Not even then."

He patted her head. "You are a good daughter."

"Father . . ." she started to say, but he was gone. She went inside. As she dressed, her fingers moved turgidly. Which was this? Still the dream? Sitting on the floor, she drew her boots up over her calves and fastened the zippers securely. Chapel awoke and looked at her.

"I thought I heard a noise."

"I couldn't sleep." She went to the window and gazed outside. "I had the strangest dream. My father came and looked in the window. When I went out and talked to him, he brought me back here."

"Your father is dead, isn't he?" Chapel said.

"How did you know that?"

"I've seen your psychological profile. I suppose I shouldn't have told you. It makes most people feel uncomfortable."

"I don't mind. He is dead. That's what made it seem so odd. In the dream, he was both alive and dead."

There was a sound. Both women stopped and listened. Uhura identified the noise at once. It was a phaser.

She and Chapel raced for the door. Outside, it was brighter than she had expected, the sky like a gray shroud. She started to run, but stopped. In the soft dust beside the door, she saw two distinct sets of footprints. One was her own bare feet. The other set was larger, firmer, and made by well-worn boots.

Chapel pushed past her and raced down the street. There were voices shouting nearby. Uhura couldn't move. It was like a dream when her feet were buried in cement and she couldn't budge. This was real, though.

A voice said, "Daughter." Cold fingers touched her arm.

18

His feet propped precariously on the edge of a win-dowsill, Kirk sat in a chair more suited to Ola's tiny frame than his own rather broad one. In at least one respect, the discrepancy pleased him; it was satisfy-ing to discover that not everything here had been ar-ranged for his convenience. Then he heard the faint hum of a phaser. Dropping his feet, he stood.

"Is something wrong, Captain?" asked Lieutenant Sulu, who was showing Ola a few additional card tricks.

"I thought I heard phaser fire."

"But who—?"

"Be quiet." The sound came again. There could be no doubting its meaning this time. "Come on. We'd better take a look."

Sulu sprang to his feet and started for the door, but had gone only a step when Ola reached out desperately and grabbed his leg. "No, don't!" she cried.

Sulu shook his foot. "Ola, let go of me. What's wrong?"

Kirk turned in the doorway. "Ola, stop that. Let him go. We'll be right back."

She released Sulu, but tears filled her eyes. "You must not," she told Kirk plaintively. "Not now—not in the dark. They will be waiting for you."

"What are you talking about?"

"The Strangers. You don't know about them. They will take you."

"It's some religious thing," Sulu said. He stood beside Kirk. "She talked about them while we were playing cards. I don't know what she means."

"I heard her, too." Kirk went toward Ola, holding out his hands. "Ola, I'm sorry, but we have to go see what's happening. We'll be back soon enough. You can stay here."

"No!" she cried, throwing herself at him.

Kirk danced away. He couldn't waste any more time arguing with her. "Come on, Mr. Sulu," he said. "Let's go."

They rushed outside. Kirk paused in the middle of the street, turning his head. He clutched his phaser in one hand. He had no idea whether it would work, but he wasn't about to test it now. If it didn't work, he'd just as soon not know. There was a certain confidence to be gained from being ignorant.

"Look, Captain," said Sulu. "Down the street. There's someone there."

Kirk looked down the street past the house Uhura and Chapel occupied. He saw what appeared to be four men: two crouched in the dust, while two more lay on their backs. Holding his phaser in front of him, Kirk moved cautiously in that direction. Sulu walked beside him.

The security men, Boggs and Kaplan, emerged half-dressed from their house. Kirk waved them back. "Stay here," he said, "and keep us in sight."

Chapel came running from her house. "Captain Kirk, what's wrong? I heard phaser fire."

"Get behind us. There may be trouble ahead."

But he had gone only a short distance when he thought he recognized one of the crouching figures. The pointed ears made identification simple. "Spock, is that you?"

"It's all right, Jim." It wasn't Spock who answered,

but Kirk knew the voice: Dr. Leonard McCoy. "The trouble's over."

Kirk quickened his pace. Turning, he waved at Boggs and Kaplan, indicating it was all right for them to come ahead.

Kirk reached Spock and McCoy before anyone else. He glanced at the bodies in the dust. He knew only one of them.

"What's Clayton doing here? Who's this other man?"

Spock stood up, leaving the injured men in the care of Dr. McCoy. "I had to knock Mr. Clayton unconscious. The other was struck by phaser fire."

"Whose?"

"Clayton's."

"How did he get hold of a phaser?"

"He took it—stole it on the *Enterprise*."

Reaching down, Kirk retrieved a phaser from the dust. "Is this it here?"

"I believe so, yes."

Kirk tucked the phaser in his belt. "Now, who's this other one?" he asked, leaning over to see. The man wore a Star Fleet uniform, but Kirk didn't recognize him from the *Enterprise*. Besides, the insignia on his tunic was one Kirk could not identify.

"This man and several others tried to follow us through the village. When he made his presence known, Clayton opened fire with the phaser. This man fell, but the others apparently managed to escape."

"He's not dead?"

"Dr. McCoy says no."

"He must be from down here."

"Apparently so."

McCoy stood up. "We ought to take these men somewhere. Neither's hurt seriously, but they need time to recover."

"I've never seen that insignia before," Kirk said, pointing.

"Nor have I, Captain," said Spock, "but I believe it's the *Rickover*."

"Are you sure of that?"

Kirk whistled softly. He pointed to the bodies. "Kaplan, Boggs, Sulu, let's move these men."

McCoy and Kaplan raised Clayton off the ground, while Sulu and Boggs carried the other man. Kirk thought he looked incredibly thin and frail. He couldn't have weighed more than a hundred pounds.

Kirk let Nurse Chapel step past, then fell behind to walk with Spock. "Well, Mr. Spock, maybe you'd better tell me what goes on. I seem to recall leaving explicit instructions for you to remain aboard the *Enterprise*."

"It wasn't my idea, Captain, I assure you. Clayton stole a phaser and forced Dr. McCoy and me to accompany him here. Apparently we were his hostages."

"Do you know why he did it?"

"Perhaps he will explain when he regains consciousness."

"I hope so, but so far, with Thomas, we haven't learned very much useful."

Kirk followed the others into the nearest lighted house, the one Chapel and Uhura occupied. Despite the commotion, the other houses remained as dark and silent as ever. Kirk didn't like that. Curiosity, he believed, was a universal characteristic of intelligence.

Inside, Clayton and the other men lay on the floor. There were soft furs under their backs.

"What do you think, Bones?" Kirk said. "Ten minutes? Twenty? When will they come around?"

"It's difficult to say definitely with Clayton. Spock could tell you more about Vulcan nerve pinch than I could. As for the other one, give him twenty minutes at the most."

"Fine. We'll wait." Kirk waved his arms expansively at the interior of the house. "Gentlemen, make yourselves at home," he told Spock and McCoy. "Welcome to Lyra."

"Captain Kirk," Lieutenant Sulu said, "I've been thinking. As long as we're going to stay here, couldn't I go next door and get Ola?"

"Yes, do. I'd forgotten about her."

"Ola, I believe, is the Lyran female," said Spock.

"Yes. She stayed in the house when Sulu and I ran out. Apparently she's afraid of the dark."

"That seems to be a common tendency here. On our way through the streets, we passed no natives."

"It is beginning to get a good deal brighter now." Following Sulu, Kirk stepped outside. Glancing at the sky, he waited for Sulu to cover the short distance separating the two houses. Then he reached into his belt and removed the phaser he had earlier retrieved. This was the weapon Clayton had used to stun the other man. Kirk pointed the phaser at a forty-five-degree angle to the sky and pressed the firing mechanism. Nothing happened. No hum. No bolt of energy. No flash of power. He checked the control, switched to a different setting, and fired again. Still, nothing. With a sigh Kirk lowered his arm. Didn't anything make sense on this world?

For several long moments Kirk stood alone outside the house, watching the sky as it grew progressively brighter, and the shadow of the moon as it moved relentlessly onward.

Then he heard Spock's voice from inside. "Captain Kirk, I have a signal from the *Enterprise*."

With a last look at the advent of this strange dawn, Kirk turned and went into the house. He took the communicator from Spock and said, "Kirk here."

He was answered by an outburst of excited babbling. It had to be Scotty, he guessed, grinning. When he got frantic, the ship's engineer often neglected to keep his brogue under proper control.

"Hey, Scotty, slow down," Kirk said. "Everyone's fine down here. Everyone's perfectly okay."

"Well, thank the Lord of the Cosmos for that, Captain Kirk. I've been trying like a devil to raise you these past few minutes, ever since that loony escaped from sick bay and took Mr. Spock and Dr. McCoy away with him."

"I know all about that, Scotty. Spock and McCoy are both here with me right now. Why didn't you call me as soon as they beamed down?"

"But that's what I'm saying, Captain. I've been trying and trying and trying, but this damn fool communicator would give me nothing but static."

98

"It must have been a temporary malfunction. Maybe the eclipse caused it. Everything seems fine now." Another inexplicable mechanical failure, he thought. Just like the phaser.

"And there's something else, too, something I've been needing to tell you about." Scott seemed hesitant to go on.

"Well, what is it, Scotty? Did one of your engines develop a pair of wings and fly away? Whatever it is, tell me."

"Well, it's that task you assigned Ensign Chekov. He tells me you wanted a course projected for this planet that we're stuck inside of."

"That's right, Scotty. What did he say?"

"Well, sir, unless he's damnably wrong—and I've checked his figures, so I don't think so—then we're in a pack of real trouble."

"What sort of trouble, Scotty?"

"The worst imaginable, sir. Chekov says we're aimed dead ahead at a black hole. He says there's no way short of a miracle we can avoid a collision."

"When?"

"In ninety-three solar hours, ship's time."

Kirk whistled gently. It was a prophecy come true: the dark place where Lyra and all within it would be destroyed. Now he knew one thing: he knew why Princess Kyanna and Captain Kree were so eager to leave this world. The Klingons might not have the sensor capability of the *Enterprise*, but there was nothing so crude about their navigation equipment. "Look, Scotty, have Chekov go over his figures again. Tell him to start at the beginning and repeat every step. I want to be positive he's not mistaken."

"I'll tell him to get cracking at that within the minute, sir."

"And I'll talk to you later."

"Aye, sir. But Mr. Spock and Dr. McCoy—will they be returning to the ship?"

"For the time being, I think I'll keep them here

with me. We have only four days to live, I think I might be able to find a use for them."

"As you wish, Captain."

"And, Scotty . . . ?"

"Aye, sir."

"About the black hole. Keep that under your cap, if you can. There's no use worrying people pointlessly. Tell Chekov to do the same."

"I'll do that, sir."

"Kirk out." He shut down the communicator. Turning, he met Mr. Spock's gaze. "Well, what do you make of that?"

"I would venture to say", Captain, that that is most unpleasant news indeed."

"Mr. Spock," said Kirk, "you do possess a talent for understatement." He knew, as well as Spock did, what colliding with a black hole meant. Whatever else happened, one fact seemed certain: anything that fell inside a hole never emerged again—not in this same universe, anyway.

McCoy continued to give aid to the unconscious men, neither of whom as yet showed any firm signs of returning awareness. Nurse Chapel assisted him. Boggs and Kaplan stood in opposite corners of the room, hands clutching their apparently useless phasers. Lieutenant Sulu had not yet returned with Ola. Kirk looked at each of those present in the room. All had overheard Mr. Scott's message. None could be unaware of its full significance. "Well," Kirk said, as he continued to look from face to face, "what do the rest of you think? Any suggestions for getting us out of here would be richly appreciated."

Surprisingly, no one said a word. Just silence—uncomfortable silence. Even McCoy was not his usually vocal self.

"I think this one may be coming around," Nurse Chapel said a few minutes later. "Since he lives here, maybe he can help us, Captain Kirk." She knelt beside the mystery man. His eyelids fluttered; the muscles in his throat twitched.

Kirk went over and crouched down. More than ever, this man's face reminded him of a skull; his body was as frail as a skeleton.

"I'll hit him with another stimulant," McCoy said, gripping a hypodermic. He fired the needle at the man's thigh. "That ought to wake him up enough to talk."

"Thanks, Bones." Kirk leaned close to the man. "Commander," he said, using the rank shown on the man's frayed sleeve. "Commander, can you hear me?"

All at once the man's eyes came open. They were dark, old, and somehow painful to see. His jaw worked up and down. He didn't make a sound.

"Lie still," McCoy cautioned. "I am a doctor. Lie as you are. This is Captain Kirk."

The man's lips moved. Was he smiling? "You are unknown to me," he said in a flat, dead tone.

"We only reached this world a short time ago," Kirk said. "We are members of the crew of the USS *Enterprise*. Our ship was captured by this planet— by something on this planet. We must get away. Can you help us? Do you understand what's happening here?"

The man's smile widened. He shook his head slowly. "There is no such ship as the *Enterprise*."

How could Kirk argue with him? At the time of the *Rickover*, the *Enterprise* was not even a dream in its designer's deep subconscious. Who was this man? How much did he know? "That's not important," Kirk said. "What is important is that we're in trouble, every one of us in this world. We need your help. Anything you can tell me . . ."

Kirk stopped. It appeared that he was too late. The man had shut his eyes again. His chest fell and rose in a steady rhythm.

"Exhaustion," McCoy said, "and shock. I think he's fallen asleep."

"Can't you wake him?" said Kirk.

"I don't think that would be wise. This man has suffered a terrible strain."

Wearily, Kirk stood. These constant frustrations were growing harder and harder to endure. Whenever he seemed close to solving one of Lyra's mysteries, something always came up to block his success. "Well, Bones, be sure to let me know when his nap's over. It's always possible the man may be able to save all our lives." Kirk glanced at Clayton. He seemed sound asleep, too. Spock's nerve pinch had done its job. There would be no help there, either.

Sulu pushed through the doorway. Ola, trailing behind him, looked frightened half to death. Her eyes were as big as saucers and her whole body trembled. For a moment Kirk thought something else had gone wrong, but Sulu quickly reassured him. "This is the way she was when I found her, Captain. It got worse, though, when I tried to get her to come outside."

Kirk knelt down in front of the alien girl. He took her hands tightly between his. "You needn't be afraid now, Ola," he said in a patient voice. "We're all friends here. You have nothing to fear from us."

At first she seemed to believe him, but then her glance strayed past Kirk to where the two unconscious men lay. She backed away, hands to her lips, and whimpered like a frightened animal. "Strangers," she moaned. "Get them away. They have come for you."

Kirk reached out, trying to calm her, but she swatted his hand with unexpected strength. "No!" she cried. "No, they are here!"

Spinning, she broke free of Sulu's desperate grasp and ran for the doorway. Kirk tried to hurry after her, but by the time he pushed the animal skin aside and looked out, she was nowhere to be seen. He slammed his fist against the wall. The sky was a pale blue. The sun beamed brightly. Morning.

"Gone, Captain?"

Kirk turned around. It was Spock, of course. "What did you expect? You tell me. Now, what's gotten into her?"

"Perhaps Ola could answer that better than I,

Captain. She is afraid of those two men, and obviously knows who they are. Surely she could tell us a great deal we need to know."

"Maybe she could. But where is she?" Kirk turned to go back inside, then suddenly stopped. He looked up and down the street. "Now, I wonder what's become of her," he said softly.

"Ola?" asked Spock. "I assume she returned to her own home."

"Not her, no. Lieutenant Uhura. Damn it, Spock, what's wrong with me? I haven't seen Uhura since we first came out. She's gone, and I didn't even notice."

20

Like four cowboys on their way to a shootout, Kirk, Spock, Sulu, and McCoy moved side by side through the dusty streets of Tumara.

For more than an hour Kirk had led the search for Lieutenant Uhura, and when it became clear that she had utterly vanished, he'd felt there was no place left to turn. Spock had suggested their present gambit. "It appears to me," he'd said, "that the majority of this planet's ambiguities are religious in nature. Since we have no means by which to consult directly with the god, perhaps our wisest course at this time would be to seek out his nearest colleague. I suggest we visit this creature Domo. He may not know what has become of Lieutenant Uhura, but it is possible he may illuminate us in other areas."

Kirk could have kicked himself for failing to think of that before. For psychological reasons he felt a show of force was wise. Nurse Chapel remained at the house to care for the unconscious men. Kirk ordered Kaplan and Boggs to keep watch over her. The other four—Spock, Sulu, McCoy, and he—headed for Domo's house.

Now that daylight had returned, the streets of the village were crowded once more. The old Lyrans, male and female, moved with surprising haste, intent upon the accomplishment of unknown tasks. *I don't like this place*, Kirk suddenly decided. There was no laughter here, no gaiety, no pleasure in life. If this was the Garden of Eden, it was a dull, aimless, unpleasant place.

They reached the house where Domo resided without incident. As Kirk approached the door, he saw in a window a brief image of a round white face. "Ola," said Lieutenant Sulu, who had seen this face, too. "I'm sure that was her."

Kirk nodded tightly. "At least that's one mystery solved. We know where she went."

He knocked on the wooden door.

For a moment there was no response from within. Then Kirk thought he heard scraping noises, as if some heavy object were being dragged across the floor. He raised his fist to knock again. As he did, the door came open.

Domo stood in the entrance, fat, stooped, and bald-headed. He did not appear pleased to be receiving visitors at this time.

"You cannot enter the sanctum of—"

Kirk wasn't about to be stopped by nonsense. Without waiting for a formal invitation, he slipped past Domo and entered the house. Domo hesitated a moment, lips open in surprise, then bowed to the inevitable. Stepping aside, he let Spock and McCoy come through. Sulu, acting on previous instructions, remained on watch outside.

Closing the door, Domo turned and placed his furry hands upon his broad belly. "To what do I owe the pleasure of such distinguished company?" If he was being sarcastic—and Kirk assumed he was—he never cracked a grin.

The room was more plushly furnished than the other houses Kirk had seen. There were several chairs, a tall stool, and a long table piled high with papers. Kirk had assumed that the Lyrans would not possess a written language. The papers were covered with tiny scribblings. Once again, common sense had failed to present an accurate picture of this world.

A wooden ladder leaned against the back wall of the room. Kirk followed the rungs to the ceiling and saw the rectangle of a trapdoor. He remembered the telescope on the roof and smiled faintly. Was the telescope Domo's way of keeping a watchful eye on Ay-nab?

Ola was nowhere to be seen. Kirk glanced at the ladder and recalled the scraping noises he had heard. Had Ola gone—or been sent—to the roof to hide?

Kirk faced Domo and thrust an angry finger at his chest. "One of my people has disappeared. She didn't walk away; she didn't wander away. Somebody must have taken her. There's something strange going on here. You've hinted about it before, I want to know what you know about Uhura's disappearance. Where is she? Who took her there?"

Domo stared at Kirk as if he were seeing a fool. "Haven't you learned that much yet? I would have thought . . . No, never mind. How dare you come here and question me? The hand of Ay-nab is hardly mine to guide."

"Look," said Kirk, "I don't care about your god. Not his hand, not his eye, not his feet. If you know where Lieutenant Uhura is, I want to be told."

"Why, the Strangers took her—obviously," Domo crossed to the tall wooden stool and plopped down. Perched up high, he resembled a plump, contented cat. "Surely you know about the Strangers, Captain. There are two of them in your own house. Ola told me she saw them there."

"Why do you call them Strangers?" Spock asked, interrupting for the first time. There was an intently curious expression on his face. He seemed to regard Domo's answer as extremely vital.

"They are Strangers because they live outside the eye of the god. They are not his children—they are different—Strangers."

"We know the men in our house did not take Uhura," Kirk said.

Domo shifted his attention back to the Captain. "Not them specifically, of course not, but there are nearly a hundred others, perhaps more. I should advise you. Keeping Strangers in your house is a dangerous practice. Others may follow and force you to the resting place before your proper time. Most likely, this is what has occurred with your friend."

Kirk couldn't decide whether Domo was being deliberately obscure or really did believe that Kirk knew more than he would admit.

Mr. Spock, interrupting again, attempted to clarify matters. "I have only just recently arrived on your world, and much of this is confusing to me. I wonder if you would mind taking a brief moment and sharing with me your knowledge of these Strangers."

Domo seemed to react well to Spock's more obsequious manner. He spoke like someone gratified by the opportunity of showing off what he knew. "Our planet, as perhaps you know, is presently partway through a journey of aeons' duration at the will of our god, Ay-nab. At the conclusion of this journey, we will reach the dark place and be destroyed. However, during the course of our quest, on many occasions alien beings have chanced upon our wandering world. In each instance, Ay-nab has claimed these creatures as his own."

"Then we are Strangers, too," said Spock.

"No," Domo said flatly. "Not you or the other ones—the Klingons. Not yet, anyway. The true Strangers are those upon whose souls Ay-nab must feed. They are dead but also alive. The Strangers seldom go out except at night, when the eye of the god is briefly hidden."

"But we will become Strangers in time? Is that correct?"

"It is fated and proper. Ay-nab is an aging god, as we are an ancient people. His substance grows weak; his light shines dimly. He needs food to survive, the strong spirit of youth, the Strangers."

Kirk had been content to let Spock lead, but the present conversation seemed to be veering from the point. He interrupted. "Where can these Strangers be found? In the daytime? When the sun is shining?"

"At the resting place," said Domo.

"And where is that?"

Domo indicated the wide world beyond the village with a sweeping wave of his hands. "It is there."

"And where exactly is there?"

"It is not for you and me to know such things. The resting place is a foul, blasphemous pit. Ay-nab knows. That is all that matters."

Domo was lying—Kirk was sure of that—but how deeply? Was anything he'd said about the Strangers true? What disturbed Kirk about Domo's explanation was how much frightening sense it seemed to make. How else could so many apparently contradictory factors be explained? The presence of Thomas Clayton. The shuttle from the *Rickover*. The officer from that same ship. The disappearance of Uhura. Ola's terrible fear of the dark.

Kirk decided to risk a long shot. If Domo knew a lot that Kirk did not, there was a distinct possibility that Kirk knew one fact of which Domo was ignorant. "Are you aware that in less than four solar days Lyra will reach the dark place and be destroyed?"

Domo's reaction left no doubt of the extent of his knowledge. His mouth hung open and his jowls shook. "You are a terrible liar," he said.

"No," said Kirk, deliberately calm. "My ship has come from space. We possess certain instruments that allow us to see ahead. There is a dark place, a black hole. Lyra is headed directly toward it."

Recovering slightly, Domo snorted. "Another lie. If such were truly the case, Ay-nab would have informed me long ago."

"Then you'd better ask him," Kirk said, "and ask

him soon. My ship is a large vessel. I am willing to take all of your people on board to save their lives. I can't do it now. I'm trapped here. If you or Aynab or anyone else knows how to set my ship free, for your own sakes you'd better tell me."

"We are fated to die because of our misdeeds. What you are suggesting is a terrible blasphemy."

"In that case," Kirk said, "we will all die together."

Domo fidgeted on the stool. His fingers twitched in his broad lap. Kirk thought Domo was a lot less eager to die than he wanted his god to think.

Kirk moved toward the door. Spock and McCoy went with him. For a brief moment Kirk paused. "Think about what I've said. I'm offering to save your life. In return, I want to know where my friend is. Cooperate with me, tell me all you know, and we'll all live better—and longer."

Domo made a weak laugh. "No one can violate the will of a god."

"Maybe we'll see about that," Kirk said.

He went outside.

Sulu, along with Spock and McCoy, waited for him. Wordlessly the four of them moved down the street. The sun beamed gorgeously in a cloudless sky. The horizon soared on all sides. Finally Kirk turned to the others. "Well, what do you think? Can he help us or can't he?"

"I think he can," McCoy said, "but that doesn't necessarily mean that he will. Domo believes in this god, even if we don't. I watched him all the time you and Spock were talking. He's afraid, Jim. He's scared to death."

"And he may have good reason," Spock said softly.

Kirk turned in surprise. "What do you mean, Mr. Spock?"

"We Vulcans have a saying, Captain. When all rational solutions refuse to fit the available facts, then seek an irrational solution that does. If the sun is a god, then most of this planet's mysteries are solved."

"But that's absurd," McCoy said.

Spock glanced toward the sky. "Is it?"

21

As soon as he reached the house, Kirk sensed that something was wrong. The animal-skin door dangled from a slender thread. A window had been shattered. And it was quiet—too quiet. He heard nothing from within.

Once inside the house, Kirk stopped and stared. There was nothing he could say, nothing he could do.

The room was an utter shambles, like the aftermath of a brawl. The few chairs lay scattered and broken. Windows were cracked, furs tossed carelessly into corners. He counted three bodies on the floor. Two, Kaplan and Nurse Chapel, were unconscious. The other, Boggs, seemed to be stirring. He rolled to a sitting position and groaned. Kirk could see dark blood on his forehead and mouth.

Neither Thomas Clayton nor the man from the *Rickover* was anywhere to be seen.

Without a word Dr. McCoy pushed past Kirk and went to Kaplan's side. Spock crouched beside the unconscious form of Chapel. He cradled her head in his lap and rubbed her temples with the tips of his fingers.

"Captain, what could have happened here?" said Lieutenant Sulu.

"I wish I knew." Kirk went over to Boggs and

111

knelt beside him. "Boggs, can you hear me?" he said.

The security man lifted his head. "They jumped us, sir. We never had a chance."

"Who jumped you, Boggs?"

"Those two crazy men, sir. We were playing a game of cards, Kaplan and I, with the deck Lieutenant Sulu let us have. I thought they were out cold, sleeping, but they must have caught us from behind when we weren't looking, Nurse Chapel tried to help. They hit her, too. I hope she's not hurt."

Kirk glanced at Spock and the injured nurse. He heard her moan gently and thought she might be coming around. "I think she'll be all right. But who did this to you? It wasn't just Clayton and the old man."

"It was, sir," Boggs insisted. "I swear it to you. If I was going to lie, I'd make up a better story than that. They don't look strong, but you could hit them and hit them and they acted like they didn't even feel it."

"Where did they go?"

"I've no idea, sir. They knocked me out. I couldn't follow them."

"All right, Boggs. I understand." Kirk stood up. "I'll have Dr. McCoy look at your wounds."

"I appreciate that, sir."

Kirk headed for the door. All at once he needed fresh air. "Sulu," he said, passing the other man, "go see if you can give Dr. McCoy a hand."

"All right, sir."

Kirk went outside. Under the warm sun, he drew several deep drafts of air into his lungs. The sense of frustration was welling up again. What an idiot I was, he thought, taking three good men to meet one overweight alien and leaving only a small force behind to deal with this. Deal with what? he asked himself. After all, objectively, there hadn't been any reason to anticipate trouble. Two crazy old men—unconscious and injured. That was all they had seemed to be. If they were more—if they were Strangers—he hadn't realized that at the time. It's not me who doesn't make sense, he decided; it's this whole damned planet. He looked up at the orb of the sun. Maybe you've got the answers, he thought, but nobody else does.

A group of figures was coming down the street toward him. It took Kirk a moment to recognize them. Why, it was Princess Kyanna and Captain Kree—the Klingons. In all that had recently happened, he'd nearly forgotten their presence here.

Kirk went forward to meet them.

Princess Kyanna, smiling and bowing, seemed relieved to see him. "Captain Kirk, what a pleasure to find you awake and well this morning," Captain Kree stood stiffly at her side.

Kirk bowed. "Princess Kyanna. What can I do for you?" Where had they been all night? he wondered. Cowering in their houses, hiding from the wrath of the Strangers?

"Don't tell me you've forgotten our agreement so soon, Captain Kirk. I promised to give you a demonstration of the weapons we found here."

"Oh, yes, the weapons. Is that one of them there?" He pointed to her hand, where she held a narrow metallic cylinder, from one end of which a tiny lever protruded like a trigger.

She nodded. "A hand device. There are others quite a bit larger, but I believe this will give you an indication of the power we possess. Interested?"

Kirk couldn't see any reason why he shouldn't be. Except, of course, that this was all so pointless. Princess Kyanna wanted him to help her escape this planet. So far, he had failed even to find a way of helping himself. "Sure, go ahead. Where do you want to go?"

"Oh, right here will be fine. Ready?"

"Whenever you are."

She raised the cylinder and pointed the solid end out over the village. Far in the distance, the skeleton of a dead tree stood against the sloping horizon. "See that?" she said.

The tree was probably a good kilometer away, perhaps even more.

"Now you see it," she said, catching her breath. One finger lightly brushed the lever at the stub of the cylinder. "And now you don't."

Kirk stared. She was right. The tree had vanished without a trace. He was impressed in spite of himself.

Princess Kyanna lowered the weapon. "Now, what about it, Captain Kirk? Do we have a deal or don't we?"

Suddenly he was looking forward to this conversation. Flatly he told her, "We don't."

She shook her head, as if unable to believe her ears. "Captain Kirk, would you say that . . . ? What are you trying to pull here?"

"I'm not trying to pull a thing. That's you, Princess, not me. You were the one who lied. You were the one who neglected to inform me that this planet is due to fall into a black hole in a few days. You were the one who forgot to let me in on the existence of the Strangers. What kind of a fool do you think I am? Was it your plan to have me solve the problem of getting out of this world and then leave me and my crew here to die?"

Kyanna's initial surprise had turned to cold anger. She glared at him with eyes that could kill. Captain Kree didn't look any happier. "None of this was any of your business, Kirk," he said.

Kirk laughed. "None of my business? The safety of my ship? The lives of my crew? I couldn't have helped you in any event. I have no more idea how to get off this planet than either of you do. There isn't an advanced species. There isn't a mysterious force. Our sensors have scanned this world up and down, over and around, a hundred times. There's nothing, Kree, except this one little village. When I die, when my crew dies, at least I'm going to have the pleasure of seeing you go with me."

Princess Kyanna made a sound in her throat like a strangled tiger. In the flash of a moment she threw up her hand. The metal cylinder gleamed in the sun. She thrust the end at Kirk's face. She jerked the trigger.

Kirk didn't have time to move a centimeter. He thought he was going to die. He had seen this weapon in operation just minutes ago. It could kill him with ease.

But nothing happened.

The weapon was dead and unresponsive in the hand of Princess Kyanna.

Kirk let out a breath of air he couldn't remember holding. "Princess Kyanna," he said softly, "if I were you, I'd think again about trying to take those weapons away from this world. Whoever owns them, whoever controls them, doesn't seem very happy at the way you're using them."

Without a backward glance, Kirk turned and headed toward the house.

Halfway there, he looked back. The Klingons had already gone.

Well, he thought with some degree of pleasure, that was one problem settled. He wondered how much of Princess Kyanna's story had ever been true. Those fantastic weapons. If she had managed to steal them, who would have borne the brunt of their use? A usurping Klingon emperor, as she claimed, or, as Kirk had all along suspected, the United Federation of Planets?

He was about to step into the house when the sound of his name made him stop. "Captain Kirk," said a soft voice. Turning, he saw Ola's round face peering at him from around the corner of the house. He went over to her.

"What are you doing here?"

"Captain Kirk," she said in a barely audible whisper, "I must speak with you."

"Is something the matter?"

"No. Please . . ." She tugged at his sleeve. "Not here." Her head twisted toward the sky. "Come with me."

He let her lead him around to the rear of the house. Back there, she pointed to a slight indentation in the rear wall, where the tile roof jutted out, producing a thin shadow. "In here," she said, crouching down.

Kirk knelt beside her. He thought he understood why she had brought him here: this must be one of the few places in the village where the perpetual noonday sun failed to shine.

"What do you want, Ola?"

"Captain Kirk," she said breathlessly, "when you came and spoke with Domo, I was there. I heard what you said to him."

"I know. I thought I saw you."

"He made me go to the roof, but I lay with my ear against the wood. You told Domo the dark place was very near. Captain Kirk, was that a lie you told?"

"I'm afraid it's the truth, Ola."

"Domo did not believe you."

"How do you know?"

"He told me afterward."

"But you don't want to die, do you, Ola?"

"No, Captain Kirk. I am very afraid. I have never had a husband. Now I never will."

"Maybe, if you help me, I can save you."

"That is why I came to you now. I want to help you, Captain Kirk."

"How, Ola?"

"The resting place. I know where to find it."

He had hoped that she would be willing to help him in other ways, but at least this was a beginning. It was imperative that he find Lieutenant Uhura. "All right, Ola, tell me."

She shook her head. "It is difficult to tell. I will have to take you there." Kirk remembered the fear she had shown in the presence of the Strangers and understood the immensity of what she was offering.

"When can you do it?"

"Now, if you wish."

"Is it better in the daytime?"

"Oh, much better. The Strangers will be in the resting place then. Ay-nab cannot see them there."

"I can't go alone." He started to stand.

She grabbed his arm. "No, please. You don't understand. This is a terrible blasphemy. Since you are my proper husband, Ay-nab may forgive me. You must go alone."

Kirk saw there was no way he could convince her otherwise. "Can I at least tell my friends where I'm going?"

She nodded, glancing fearfully at the sky. "But do it inside. Talk to them in the house. Please, Captain Kirk."

He promised that he would.

22

As she followed her father down the gentle slope of the last hill, across the bridge that spanned the creek, and then out across the broad grassy meadow, Lieutenant Uhura remembered how it had been when she was only a child, how similar to this the experience had been; it was like a slice of past time lived anew. Then, too, her father had taken her away. She remembered the strength of his big hairy hand engulfing hers, his broad-ranging steps forcing her to trot like a pony to keep pace. Odd. She hardly ever recalled such childhood memories; she thought they had vanished long ago. Except through the medium of late-night dreams, and this wasn't that; this wasn't a dream. It felt like one. Her head whirled dizzily. Her eyes refused to focus. A sudden, overwhelming smell, taste, or touch rose up to obliterate everything else. It was odd, all right. Very, very odd.

"We'll go home," he said, past a shoulder. She hurried to keep pace with his long steps. "You belong with me, not them. We are strangers here. Not like those stinking, sinning apes who live in the village."

She tried to explain about Captain Kirk. About Mr. Spock, too, and Sulu and Scotty and the rest. They were her friends. Stinking, sinning apes? Whom did he mean?

118

But it was just like a dream. Her thoughts balked, refusing to be transformed into words. The heels of her black boots sank to the soles in the soft dirt. Her skirt flapped in the breeze above tautly muscled thighs. Suddenly she laughed. It felt so good. But what?

The time she had started to recall, the time her father had taken her away like this, he had come home more often then. She was seven or eight years old. Without warning he had arrived at their city apartment one afternoon and told her mother, "I think she ought to see where we were born," and then driven the jeep through muddy roads into a deep forest, where she suffered expectant visions of lions, elephants, giraffes, and leopards, the unspoiled Africa of a child's picture book, not the gleaming glass city of Dakar that she knew so well. But the village, when they reached it, proved to be an even more puzzling place, where the men walked about in rainbow-colored robes and pillbox hats, and the women wore cotton gowns—many had veils—and the children kept hidden most of the time; she saw only a few all the time she was there. Her father, braking the jeep, leaned over and said, "I was born in this village and never saw Dakar until I was seventeen." He brought her inside to meet his brother, a huge man with gnarled arms and a wispy beard; his sister, lovely and rawboned like a wood carving; his uncle, a flat-faced man with wrinkled eyes; and his father, as thin as a ghost among giants. For more than a week she lived with his people. Her aunt took her each day into broad fertile fields, and they returned each evening at dusk to prepare the meal the men ate in one hut and the women in another.

Remembering this as she walked, Uhura breathed the nectar-sweet air of the meadow. The forest rose in front of them. It was a different place from what she remembered. They had come by a different route this time.

As a child, after visiting her father's family in the village, she never feared the forest again, or regarded it, as most city dwellers did, as a dreadful place inhabited by monsters and demons and restless, wandering spirits. Still, she had never gone there a second time. The last night of her visit, lying awake, she had overheard loud angry voices from the adjoining hut. She heard her father cry, "Superstitious fools! The Galaxy," he said, "is man's proper domain. Don't you understand about the Earth? Don't you know what it is? The Earth is a miserable, stinking cesspool filled with corpses too ignorant to die." Later, she heard him shout again: "Allah be damned! Don't give me that old nonsense. What do I care for the lies of a so-called prophet responsible for the murders of tens of thousands of innocents? Maybe that's all well enough for you," he said, "but I demand more sanity from my existence." She didn't know what he meant.

(Later she learned that her father's family, like most citizens of Senegal, followed the way of Islam, while her father himself despised all religious practices. Even in Dakar, during the moments of the day when everyone else prayed, her father walked defiantly through the kneeling bodies as though they did not exist.)

In the morning, when it was time to leave, only her aunt came to say good-bye. Leaning over, she spoke to her brother in a whispering voice not meant to be overheard. To Uhura, at that impressionable age, all of this merely constituted additional evidence of the mysteries of the adult world. Only later did she understand that that vaguely overheard argument during the night had constituted a final barrier between her father and the family he had once loved.

Here, now, on this much different world, her father spoke to her of another god. His tone was different, too, reverent, frightened. Still, consumed by her own memories, she barely heard a word. He told her that Ay-nab lived in the sky and that they must hurry, for when Ay-nab became hungry, he would wish to feed, and if they were caught in the open, he would surely select them as his prey. She did not understand. They had entered the forest. There was a hole in the ground. "Here." He pointed. "Down we go."

She kept her hand in his. They went down a ladder. There was a concrete cave. Bright torches illuminated the way. Her father moved with certain feet. The floor slanted down, but the ceiling climbed higher, until eventually even the torches failed to show it. Down, down, down—into the heart of the world. This planet didn't have a heart. It was called Lyra and it was hollow. If they went too far, they might emerge on the other side. She tried to warn her father. There were voices ahead.

They stopped in a cavern as big as a ballroom. People were everywhere. Aliens, too. She saw a Vulcan female, two Romulans, several Klingons. Nobody spoke to her. Some of the aliens she had never seen before, even in holograms. Everyone was old.

She slept in the cavern. The torches never stopped burning. Her father told her to go out into the forest. A kindly old man promised to show her the way. Together they picked fruit off the trees, until the old man went too high and the sun hurt his eyes and he fell off the branch and hit the ground and lay squirming. Frightened, she ran away into the forest. She was lost. A voice spoke in her head. It said, *I am Ay-nab, god of this world.* She lay on her back on the ground and let the warm rays of the sun touch her. Later, when she stood, she felt weak and drained, as if she had lost blood. Her father came and got her. She went with him back to the cavern. She saw the man who had fallen out of the tree. When she asked if he was all right, he said, "I, too, have fed my god."

Time passed. Her father ceased speaking directly to her. A man named Clayton said that she must learn not to desire escape. "The will of the god is an iron chain," he said. "It can be neither bent nor broken."

She did not desire escape. She was warm, never cold, contented, never sad. She slept.

When she awoke, a man had hold of her arm. He waved a stick in the air. "If any of you try to prevent me from taking her, I swear I'll break you in two with my bare hands."

"Captain Kirk," she said.

"Uhura. Thank God you know me. What have they done to you? What in hell is this place?"

She couldn't answer. This was just the resting place. She smiled. "Ay-nab fed upon my soul. I served the god well."

The man pulled her arm until she stood beside him. "I'm getting you out of here," he said.

23

Ola, trembling, grabbed his sleeve and pointed to a recess in the ground ahead. "There it is, Captain Kirk," she said. "That is the resting place of the Strangers."

Their journey had taken Kirk over familiar terrain. The rolling hills, the stream and bridge, the grassy meadow. At that point, Ola swerved in a different direction. This was a darker part of the forest, with trees stacked tightly together, flashes of sun less frequent. They had penetrated perhaps half a kilometer's depth into the forest when Ola indicated the dark recess.

Kirk covered the remaining ground quickly. The recess turned out to be a round gaping hole. Kneeling, Kirk felt inside the hole. The sides were smooth. Concrete, he guessed, the creation of an intelligent mind. He felt something hard and metallic jutting from the side. The top rung of a ladder? Stretching, he felt farther down. Yes, a ladder. Leaning over, he peered inside. Far down, he thought he saw a faint glimmer of light.

"The Strangers live in there?" he asked Ola.

She nodded. "The Strangers fear the god. They cower from his watchful eye."

"And come out at night?"

"To Tumara, yes. Some say they roam more freely here in the forest."

"You have no idea what's at the bottom of this hole?"

"You will go down there?" The thought of descent seemed to frighten her.

"It's what I came for." Kirk flipped open the communicator and called the *Enterprise*. "Scotty, Kirk here. I want you to fix my present position. I've found a vertical shaft. Ola says Uhura may be at the bottom of it."

"You're going down, sir?"

"If she's there, I've got to bring her out."

"I wish you had a phaser."

"I do, but it's not likely to function."

"If I could make a suggestion, sir, perhaps a rock or stick would serve as well."

Kirk thought that was a good idea. He switched off the communicator and went in search of a tree branch. He found one approximately the length of his arm. It seemed strong enough and straight enough. Using the knife from his utility belt, he whittled one end to a sharp point. The makeshift spear wasn't likely to kill anything bigger than a kitten, but he liked the feel of the weapon in his hand.

Next, he called Spock and told him where he was going. Ola stared in amazement at the apparent presence of a disembodied voice in Kirk's hand.

Spock was cautious. "I wish you could be certain Lieutenant Uhura is indeed there."

"I'm as sure as I'm going to be."

"Unfortunately, you have only the word of the female."

"Do you see an alternative, Mr. Spock?"

"I would suggest, now that you've located the shaft, beaming down a security team to undertake the actual assault."

Kirk knew Spock was only thinking practically. "No. For whatever it's worth, I gave Ola my word. Besides, since our phasers don't work, one man ought to be able to function better alone. Give me a reasonable period of time. If I'm not back by then, send a security team."

"I'll head the assault personally."

Kirk nodded. Spock was the sort of person who revealed his friendship in pragmatic ways. "I appreciate your concern, Mr. Spock. With any luck, it won't be necessary."

Kirk signed off. He waited a few more minutes until Scotty called to verify that he had successfully fixed Kirk's present position. Kirk thanked him, signed off, and attached the communicator to his belt. If this shaft was part of what he thought it was, the communicator would not likely be of much use to him once he began to descend.

"I'm going now," he told Ola.

"And me?" she asked. "I will go, too?"

Kirk shook his head. He appreciated how much of an effort it took for her to make such an offer. She was already trembling in anticipation. "That's not necessary, Ola. I can find my way from here alone."

A trickle of tears formed in her eyes. He could tell from her expression that she did not expect to see him again.

He went over and took her hands in his. "I want to thank you, Ola, for all that you've done for me. I only hope, somehow, this works out the best for you."

She nodded slowly, struggling to smile. "You saved my life, too, Captain Kirk."

"That was nothing, Ola. That was easy." He patted the furry crest of her head. "What you've done has been much harder."

"Good . . . good-bye, Captain Kirk."

"Good-bye, Ola."

He went to the hole and swung a foot over the edge. Finding a foothold on the top rung of the ladder, he commenced his descent. The shaft was sufficiently wide to permit his body to move freely. The rungs were spaced so that his foot automatically found the next. The creatures who had constructed this shaft were likely of human size. Did that eliminate Ola's own people? Evolution sometimes tended to work rapid changes. On a world like Lyra, with the weather under strict control, a structure like this might endure for hundreds of thousands of years.

As he moved down the ladder, Kirk kept a watchful eye pointed below. The faint glimmer of light he had observed from above grew progressively bigger and brighter. Torchlight, he decided, from the way it flickered. When he reached the bottom of the shaft, he saw that he was right. He stood in a low-ceilinged chamber. The flame of the torch licked high at the concrete wall. Looking up the shaft, he saw only a circle of blue sky; the sun itself did not show here. A horizontal tunnel branched off from the chamber. There was no other way to go. Clutching his spear, Kirk set off down the tunnel.

Additional torches appeared at intervals of a dozen meters to help show him the way. He kept a watchful eye for side passages that might later cause confusion, but the main tunnel continued to run uninterrupted. The ceiling climbed higher until eventually he could no longer see it. He walked softly in an attempt to minimize the sound of his own boots. Frequently he stopped and listened, hoping to catch any stray sounds of life ahead.

Kirk estimated he had followed the tunnel for a quarter of a kilometer before he first heard something from ahead. The sounds were as yet indistinct, but he slowed his pace and moved on the balls of his feet. The Strangers. It had to be. What else could be found down here?

But what were the Strangers? Even if he eliminated the religious elements from what Domo had told him, what remained was still a puzzle. A wandering planet like Lyra might well attract a certain amount of outside attention. In the course of twenty years' time, three Federation vessels—the *Rickover*, Clayton's ship, and the *Enterprise*—had chanced upon this world. But Domo claimed the Strangers numbered more than a hundred. Where had the others come from? An old-style starship like the *Rickover* carried a crew of fewer than forty; Clayton had been alone. Kirk couldn't begin to speculate. The sounds ahead were clearer now. He thought he could make out voices. He stepped softly. There was a bend in the tunnel. He went around it, then stopped.

A cavern as big as a ballroom gaped in front of him. Kirk knew at once what he had found: the resting place of the Strangers. There were a hundred or more. Some were asleep, some sat motionlessly on the concrete floor, a few wandered aimlessly. The voices he had heard belonged to creatures talking to themselves. Kirk could identify most of the beings present. There were humans, Vulcans, Klingons, Romulans, Tholians. Several of the aliens, however, were totally unknown to him. Tightening his grip on the stick in his hand, Kirk edged into the chamber.

He went unnoticed. Growing bolder, he moved among the Strangers. Still no one tried to stop him. He hadn't seen Uhura yet. Far across the chamber, he spotted Thomas Clayton. Clayton met his glance and looked straight back. There was no immediate recognition in his gaze.

Kirk limited his search to those Strangers wearing Star Fleet uniforms. Almost all of these seemed to be members of the *Rickover* crew. Finally he found Uhura. Apparently asleep, she lay curled against a wall. Her uniform was torn. She was bare-legged. Reaching down, Kirk gently shook her arm. "Uhura, wake up. It's me—Captain Kirk."

Her eyes opened at once. She stared blankly at him.

His voice had attracted attention. Several of the Strangers began to edge toward him. They moved like shambling zombies. He had to assume their intent was hostile. He held his stick high in the air. "If any of you try to prevent me from taking her, I swear I'll break you in two with my bare hands."

Kirk hoped it was more than an empty threat. In spite of their numbers, the Strangers seemed too frail to put up much of a fight, more like ghosts than men or beasts. Still, Kirk remembered what had happened to Kaplan and Boggs.

His voice seemed to have an effect on Lieutenant Uhura. She shook her head slowly. "Captain Kirk," she said, as if she were learning his name for the first time.

"Uhura." He clutched her arm tightly. "Thank God you know me. What have they done to you? What in hell is this place?"

She didn't answer right away. She smiled. "Ay-nab fed upon my soul. I served the god well."

He didn't have time to consider her meaning. The Strangers formed a circle around him. Kirk jerked Uhura to her feet. "I'm getting you out of here."

She didn't resist. Pulling her behind him, Kirk headed for the crowd. He waved his stick. The circle drew back. He thrust with the point. There was an opening. He went through it. The Strangers turned, following him with blank eyes. This was less difficult than he had feared. Who were these creatures? Why didn't they try to stop him?

Suddenly a grinning face loomed in front of him. It took Kirk a moment to recognize Thomas Clayton. He held up his stick. Clayton grabbed his wrist in a tight grip. "Kirk, you fool," he said. "Don't you know you can't escape the eye of a god?"

With a furious jerk Kirk freed his arm. He swung at once. The stick cracked Clayton solidly on the side of his head. He tottered for a long moment, then fell. He wasn't bleeding. Kirk went around him.

After that, no one tried to interfere. As soon as he reached the mouth of the tunnel, Kirk gave Uhura a hard shove. "Run!" he shouted. She stood fast. He pushed her again. "Dammit, I said run!"

She moved at a slow trot. Kirk kept pace with her.

The torches swept past. Kirk felt like a figure trapped in a dream, a slow-motion runner. Uhura never said a word. Kirk kept his ears open for pursuit. He thought he heard the patter of feet behind. It wasn't more than one or two persons. Clayton again? No, he was out for good. Kirk took Uhura's hand and tried to get her to move faster. Oblivious of him, she maintained the same plodding pace.

When they reached the open place at the bottom of the vertical shaft, Kirk pointed to the foot of the ladder and told Uhura to start climbing. Her lips moved, but he couldn't understand a word. He thought she was mumbling senselessly. He pointed to the ladder again. "Climb," he said. "Get up there. Get moving."

This time she obeyed. She moved gingerly because of her bare feet, Kirk followed.

As he climbed, he could hear her better. "Ay-nab," he heard her say. "My god." He thought she might be praying. For what? he wondered. She wasn't the same woman he had known. What had been done to her back there? Would she ever be normal again?

When they reached the top of the ladder and stepped into the clear light, Uhura fell to her knees and wept like a child. Kirk peered down the shaft. He was sure someone was climbing up after them. Who? He couldn't see clearly enough to tell. He made Uhura come to her feet. "We've got to go," he said. "I'm taking you home." As he spoke, he put his lips close to her ear, as if she were deaf.

He didn't think she knew him. He shoved her toward the woods. "That way," he said, hoping he remembered the correct path.

"Captain Kirk?"

He looked up. Ola emerged from the shelter of a plump tree. He was surprised and happy that she had waited for him. "Ola, am I ever glad to see you."

"Is this the friend you sought?" Ola came to within a few meters of Kirk and Uhura but stopped there.

"Don't you remember? This is Lieutenant Uhura. I found her down there with the Strangers."

"She is not the same," she said flatly. "She is one of the Strangers now."

"I know," Kirk said. "We've got to get her home. Will you help?"

"Yes. But how can I?" Ola took another hesitant step forward. It was plain she was scared to death of Uhura. "Ay-nah has taken part of her soul."

Kirk didn't have time to unravel the meaning of her words. He told Ola he thought someone might be following them. He asked her to lead the way back to Tumara.

She continued to wrestle with her fear. "This is the way we came," she said, edging past Uhura and pointing to a narrow path between two tall trees.

"Then that's the way we'd better go." Kirk tried to get Uhura to follow. Once more he had to pull her arm to get her to move. They had to walk. The forest was too thick to make running safe. Kirk didn't like any of this. Maybe Dr. McCoy could bring Uhura around. The trouble was, Kirk couldn't tell what was wrong with her. Maybe Ola knew. Or Domo. When they reached the village, he would question both of them. It was impossible to tell whether someone was still following them. Kirk somehow sensed that they weren't alone. There was a presence in the forest behind. He didn't like that, either. Ola sensed it, too. She kept glancing over her shoulder. She moved with long, frightened strides.

Reaching the edge of the forest, they moved onto the meadow. They had gone only a hundred meters when Kirk saw a running figure emerge from the forest and start after them. It looked like a tall, thin, black-skinned man with a crown of white hair.

"Daughter!" he shouted. "Daughter, don't leave me!"

Kirk didn't understand. Before he could do anything, Uhura suddenly cried out. Jerking away from Kirk, she raced toward the approaching man.

Kirk started to go after her. All at once Ola was in front of him. She held up her hands. "No, Captain Kirk, don't. It's them, don't you see? We must run, or they will take you, too."

"I'm sorry, Ola. She's my friend." He pushed her gently aside and ran after Uhura. Who was this man? One of the Strangers, yes, though Kirk could not recall seeing him in the cavern. He had called Uhura "daughter." That couldn't possibly be true. Could it?

Kirk caught up with Uhura just as she reached the man. He never hesitated. Something told him if he didn't strike now, he might never be given a second chance. He raised his stick. He started to bring it down. The sun struck his eyes. For a moment he was blinded. His arm was heavy and turgid. He couldn't swing the stick. His muscles were frozen. He couldn't budge.

Face distorted by fury, the man leaped at Kirk. His fingers came up like claws. Kirk knew he couldn't fight back. There was a sharp pain at his throat. He couldn't breathe. He gasped, then gagged. A dark face, creased by age, swam in front of his eyes. He heard Uhura. She made a sound like a cat's purr. Kirk struggled to move. He couldn't. The sun pounded at his head. He knew he could be dying.

Then, suddenly, it was over. Air rushed into his lungs. His hands fell to his sides. He realized that the man's face had gone away. Distantly, someone was crying.

Slowly Kirk's vision cleared. Regaining his senses, he looked down. The man who had attacked him lay in the grass. There was a rock beside his head.

Something warm and furry and frightened leaped into his arms. It took a long second for Kirk to realize that it was Ola. "You saved my life," he cried, hugging her to him. "You threw a rock, didn't you?"

Uhura sat slumped on the ground. She was the one he had heard crying.

As he embraced Ola, Kirk's eyes moved involuntarily to the sky. He saw the orb of the sun. He remembered something: that terrible weight in his arm. It wasn't possible, was it? The sun hadn't really tried to kill him?

24

On the way back to Tumara, Kirk stopped only long enough to call Scott on the *Enterprise* and Spock in the village to tell them that he had found Lieutenant Uhura and was returning with her. Spock reported that during Kirk's absence a shaken Domo had appeared at the house.

"What's bothering him?" Kirk asked.

"He says he has spoken to his god."

"About the black hole?"

"Yes. Apparently the god confirmed what you told him at the meeting. I can't imagine what else would frighten him so much."

"Has he any suggestions for a practical solution to this mess?"

"That would be hard to say, Captain. At the moment, I fear, he's too upset to communicate intelligibly."

"Then let him alone till I arrive. It won't hurt to give him time to think about what lies ahead for all of us."

"As you wish, Captain."

When Kirk arrived at the house, everyone was present. As soon as he guided Lieutenant Uhura through the doorway, Dr. McCoy hurried over and eased her down onto the furs. He examined her quickly. "There's no sign of any physical damage, Jim, but

133

she's definitely suffering from shock. I can give her a sedative, if you won't be needing her."

"No, go ahead." Ola had followed him inside. She stood with her back against the wall, staring across the length of the room at the squat figure of Domo, who crouched in one corner. "Is something wrong?" Kirk asked her.

She pointed a finger. "You must talk to him. You must make him help you."

She meant Domo. Kirk agreed with her evaluation. Crossing the room, he loomed above the Lyran. "I understand you want to talk to me," Kirk said.

Domo lifted his head, as if surprised to discover that he was not alone. "Captain Kirk, I told my god that I did not wish to die. I told him it was wrong to punish me for the misdeeds of those long dead. He turned a deaf ear. He showed no mercy. He said those who accept favors must also accept misfortunes. I do not want to die."

"Neither do any of us," Kirk said. "But how can I help?"

"You spoke of your ship," Domo said eagerly. "You said you could take all of us to a new world of our own. The god could not follow us there. We would be free of his terrible eye."

Kirk shook his head slowly. "I can't, Domo, as long as my ship is trapped here. Can you release it?"

Domo looked stricken. Apparently he had forgotten that the Enterprise could not go anywhere at the moment. "Not I," he said, shaking his head sadly.

"Only Ay-nab can free your ship."

"I know that," Kirk said. In the meadow he had learned something that had altered his past thinking about this world. He now knew that Ay-nab did indeed exist. He had seen him and felt him. "But there must be something you can do. You claim you talk to Ay-nab. You're our only hope, Domo. If he's determined to kill us, only you can force him to change his mind."

Dr. McCoy, frowning, moved away from the now

unconscious Lieutenant Uhura. "Jim, you can't be serious. Ay-nab is a star. It's not alive."

"I believe that it is, Bones. Don't ask me to explain it. There's a force present on this planet—an unseen entity—and a damnably powerful one, too. I'll explain to you later how I know. It may be a sun, and it may not be. I don't think that's what's important. It exists—and it's what's holding us here."

"Tentatively, I must agree with Captain Kirk," Mr. Spock said. He moved slowly across the room. "Ever since I first reached this world, I have sensed the presence of something very old and very powerful. As you know, we Vulcans are considerably more adept telepathically than most humans. Perhaps that is a logical explanation."

"And you never thought to mention this before?" McCoy said angrily.

"I had no proof, Doctor, only my own senses. Apparently Captain Kirk has discovered something more definite."

Kirk wasn't about to explain that his own evidence was no more definite than Spock's. He believed it. That was what mattered. "Domo," he said, "it's up to you. The rest of us can do nothing. If you want to live, you'll have to speak to Ay-nab."

"No, not him."

Kirk spun at the interruption. It was Ola. "What do you mean?" he asked her.

"I mean, Captain Kirk, that Domo is not the only one who can speak to the god. Look at him. He is too old, too afraid. I will speak to the god. I, Captain Kirk, and you. We will go together."

Domo started to make a protest, but Kirk cut him off short. "Ola, do you know how?"

"I do," she said firmly. "I have watched Domo. I know his techniques. I can speak to the god, and so can you."

"Captain," Spock said, "with all due respect, perhaps I ought to be the one who tries, not you. As a student of Vulcan mind-touch techniques, I am intimately acquainted with the intricacies of telepathic communication. I may find it easier to establish contact with this being."

Kirk shook his head. He knew what Spock said made sense, but the expression on Ola's face was enough to tell him that this time he would have to go himself. "If I fail, I'll want you to try, Mr. Spock. This first time, though, I think it ought to be me who goes."

"As you wish, Captain."

Ola went to the doorway and stood. Her feet danced nervously, as if she were unable to stand in one place. Domo watched her. His face seemed more tired than ever. Kirk wondered if the old priest even had the energy to stand. "We must not delay," Ola said.

Kirk smiled at her sudden impatience. Apparently he was not the only one who had learned something on the meadow. He faced his crew. "I'm going to Domo's house. You all know where that is. Give me no more than three hours. Keep in close contact with Mr. Scott all the while. If I'm not back in that time, if you haven't heard from me by then, Mr. Spock should come alone to see what's happened."

"And if you fail?" McCoy said. It was not a possibility Kirk had wished to consider.

He smiled suddenly. "Then, Bones, I guess we're all going to find out what it's like to fall inside a black hole."

25

The techniques Ola showed Kirk to facilitate rapid mental contact with the god were not unfamiliar to him. Empty the mind. Relax the body. Obliterate memory. In the end, what they came down to was nothing more complex than simple meditation. While he was by no means as adept as Spock at the practice, he did know the proper exercises to follow.

So he sat on the floor in Domo's house, with his arms folded on his chest, his legs crossed beneath him, his head thrown back at a sharp angle, and his mind as much of a blank as he could make it.

In this state of consciousness, time had little meaning. Seconds, minutes, hours, days, weeks, months, and years—all felt quite the same. Ola sat beside him. He no longer recognized her existence.

It started with a tickle he couldn't scratch.

The reason he couldn't scratch the tickle was that it wasn't on his skin: it was in his mind.

The tickle started small but grew. Soon it wasn't a tickle: it was a presence. Something outside his mind. Just beyond the surface. Circling. Circling slowly.

Ay-nab? thought Kirk, focusing his mental energy on the one word. He never made a sound. The language that he used was in no sense a collection of

137

sequential symbols. Kirk made use of the truly universal language inherent within all intelligent beings: the language of thought. *Ay-nab, I feel you near. Come closer. We must speak.*

Hearing him or not, the presence did grow stronger. Kirk could see it clearly: a round, pulsating ball of fire. Like a sun, he thought, a star.

A voice reached him soundlessly: *I am Ay-nab, god of this world, who bathes it in the light and heat that is his to share.*

He replied: *And I am James Kirk of the United Federation of Planets. A man. A human being.*

You dare to approach me?

I do. I come to seek mercy for all those who must soon perish at the dark place. I ask you to free my ship so that we may avoid a disaster that is not our doing.

Ay-nab laughed, a terrible, mocking sound. Kirk grabbed hold of his head. He couldn't bear this. (But he knew that he must.)

Ignorant mortal, said the god. *Fool. You dare to speak to me of mercy? What do you know? What have you seen of the cosmos? I am Ay-nab. I am all-knowing, all-seeing, all-powerful. I am eternal. Here—observe for yourself. I, Ay-nab, will reveal who deserves to perish.*

The blinding ball of fire shrank to the size of a pinpoint. In its place Kirk saw a series of visions, like separate clicking photographs of the past.

He saw:

A shimmering blue-green-brown planet wreathed by hovering white clouds.

Cities of glass and steel so vast that they occupied entire continents from sea to sea.

A race of white-furred bipeds with long arms and bare faces. These creatures resembled the Lyrans in the same sense that a thoroughbred resembles a nag.

Then came war.

Kirk saw:

Destruction.

Agony.

Death.

Indescribable suffering.

Phallic missiles rocketed between continents. Heat rays flashed. In a matter of hours, millions perished.

Kirk observed all of this. He was horrified. He was never shocked.

This was long ago, Kirk said calmly. *To punish your own people for the sins of their distant ancestors is to be a god without common mercy.*

But, again, Ay-nab uttered his terrible, mocking laugh. *Fool,* he said, expanding to full size and obliterating the visions, *That is but a hint of what is to come. Watch, see, observe. Only then will you know.*

The god shrank. The visions returned.

Kirk saw:

The planet rebuilt from the ashes of destruction, until not even the faintest scar remained to show the wounds of the past.

Then came a second war, this one no less terrible than the first.

And rebirth.

War.

Rebirth.

War.

And all this time, as the visions passed in procession, the god laughed. His voice echoed everywhere, drowning out the constant howls of the dying.

Seven times the cycle recurred. Seven resurrections, seven deaths.

In the end, Kirk said, *What you have shown me is not unique. Throughout the Galaxy, I have seen this pattern repeated. Even my own people did not wholly avoid it. In time, some species have managed to break the cycle—mine was one—usually by voyaging into space. Others, failing, have destroyed themselves utterly. I still say these are antique visions. Revenge* and mercy are not compatible. You must choose one.

And the god, not speaking, showed Kirk a final vision of rebirth.

See? said Kirk. It is as I said. Now the cycle has ended.

But the god laughed. No! he cried, swelling to full size, pulsating with anger. (Kirk gripped his throbbing head.) The cycle has not ended. The world, grown weary of war and death, remains poised at the brink of final obliteration.

Show me, said Kirk.

No, you have seen enough. I must first explain how at long last one wise being appeared among the savages. This creature, who had somehow managed to glimpse a portion of the cosmic truth, came to me only hours before doomsday and begged for my divine intervention. I did not refuse his request—I am not without mercy—but I demanded stringent terms. I would save his world, only to destroy it. Vengeance is mine, I told him. You have forsaken the right to eternal life.

And you saved their world?

I did. By revealing to them the means by which to create a planet where war could no longer exist. The world I gave to them is the world where you now reside.

You taught them to construct a Dyson sphere.

That is your term, I believe.

And then?

See for yourself.

Dwindling to pinpoint size, Ay-nab revealed to Kirk a vision of the great engineering project which had fashioned from the matter of a solar system a single planet encompassing its own sun.

And the people were saved, Kirk said, through your intervention.

Saved, yes, said the god, but saved to die. I had kept my side of the bargain and intended to force them to keep theirs. They were an old people now, wasted and degenerate. The great project had taken what little remained of their once vast energies. The threat of war was ended, for they were too tired to fight, content to let me do their living for them. I fed and cared for them, as any diligent parent would, but all the while I carried them through space to a certain rendezvous with the dark place where cosmic obliteration would at last claim the remnants of their race.

And yourself? Kirk said.

And myself. I am their god. If they die, I must die as well.

Can you tell me how long this voyage has lasted?

The god replied with a thought that might have been a number between two and four billion years.

Kirk admitted that he could not conceive of such a passage of time.

Many died, the god explained, and the children born were few. This huge planet, once fully populated, became an empty shell. In time, I gathered the few who remained into a single village and cared for them there. Still their number continued to decline. Now the end has at last been reached.

But what of these others, Kirk said, the ones who live underground, the Strangers?

They, too, are mere remnants. In the course of my great journey, thousands have come to this planet. All were fed and succored by me—but kept apart from my own people to avoid contamination.

Contamination of your people or by your people? Kirk asked.

Both. Ay-nab smiled. (Kirk sensed the gesture.) All mortal beings are savages content to spend their days killing one another with weapons of terrible destruction. You were nearly slain, until I chose to intervene, by one of the hundreds of weapons brought to this planet over the millennia. The Strangers themselves live in a shelter constructed by one visiting species which attempted to continue to make war up-

on another species before I chose to strike both of
them down. This was many thousands of years ago,
but all must perish in time. I decided that long ago.
Everything mortal is but a mocking image of the
gods.

Then you are not the only one, Kirk said.

I cannot speak of that.

Are all stars living beings?

That word—all—is much too vast a term to be
understood.

Then most? asked Kirk.

A mortal has no need for such knowledge.

The mark of a mortal is his intense need to ac-
quire all knowledge.

With which to destroy.

Without regard for its eventual consequences. This
may not be the wisest course, I admit, but it is the
one my species has long followed.

I have seen too much to accept such statements.

But perhaps you have still not seen enough. Let
me ask you again: do you still believe it is necessary
for all to perish?

Ay-nab seemed bewildered that Kirk had even
asked such a question. Have you seen nothing I
have shown you? he cried.

Then let me show you why I believe that you are
wrong, said Kirk.

Now it was his turn to show pictures: visions of
Earth and its people. Men helping men. People in
love. Cooperative projects. Works of music, art, and
literature. Kirk tried to present a consistent argument: there was more to existence than what this
one ancient god had witnessed. If many species failed
in large ways, many others succeeded in smaller ones.
Where the mass was wrong, the individual often was
right.

But the god scoffed at these visions. This is meager,
petty, stuff, he said.

Isn't it possible, Kirk asked, that the true substance

of life is petty?* He believed he was speaking not only for the lives of a few hundred individuals but also to justify the very nature of his own existence.

What do you want of me? the god demanded.

Only mercy.

Mercy for yourself?

No, for everyone.

Then for these, too? said the god with a sudden burst of mockery. He showed Kirk a vision of the Klingons, Captain Kree and Princess Kyanna. These who were so eager to steal the weapons of great destruction to use against your own kind?

Yes, the Klingons, too, Kirk said unhesitantly. They are a young race. Should they be refused the opportunity to learn, to break the terrible cycle of peace and war?

You seek mercy for your sworn enemies?

I ask you to spare them, yes. They and everyone else on this world.

Excluding myself? the god said mockingly. You wish to see me perish alone.

I seek only that which is possible. I ask mercy for everyone, including the Strangers. Many are human beings like myself. If I deserve to live, so do they.

Ay-nab chuckled softly, his ironic laughter (if it could be called that) even more dreadful than before. I cannot spare the dead.

The dead?

The Strangers. Apparently you have failed to understand. Those who have intruded upon my world have been used by me as a source of necessary energy to keep my own fires burning.

I do not understand.

You are a mortal. They are dead.

But I've seen them. They walk, they talk, they breathe. My medical officer, Dr. McCoy, has examined some of them. He didn't know they were dead.

And he, too, is a mortal. As long as I permit it, the Strangers mock life. When their bodies wear out, I discard them.

One of the Strangers came aboard my ship. An old friend of mine—Thomas Clayton. He said he had escaped from you.

A lie. I sent him to you. The Strangers are dead without always knowing of their true condition.

Something in that last sentence moved Kirk more deeply than anything else Ay-nab had said. Repressing a shiver of disgust, he said, *Does that include Lieutenant Uhura?*

No. *Her father took her before it was her time. I fed upon her only once, briefly. She will recover.*

And Ola? said Kirk.

Ola? She is not a Stranger. She is one of mine. I ask particular mercy for her.

Why? (With contempt.)

Because she is young.

That does not move me.

Because she can be saved.

I do not intend to perish alone.

Kirk revealed a vision of Ola saved from the Kova in the forest.

He revealed a vision of himself saved from the Stranger on the meadow.

There is more than this I could show, said Kirk. *The point is that Ola deserves to be saved. She brought me to you. She is not afraid.*

It is true that I witnessed these deeds, said the god.

And? asked Kirk.

Ay-nab was silent for a long time, and Kirk feared that he might have lost contact. He struggled to make one final plea. All at once he felt his strength fading and knew he could not remain here for long.

Then he felt a new presence. It was Ola. He realized with a start that she had been present since the beginning.

No! she cried.

Who dares to speak? said Ay-nab.

It is I, your last child—it is Ola.

And you seek mercy for yourself? the god said, laughing.

No. Not for myself. If my people deserve to die, then so do I, but if I deserve to die, then so do you. We are merely mortals. You, Ay-nab, are a god. If we have done wrong, then the source of our evil must lie within you.

Ignorant child, Ay-nab said pityingly. *You are mistaken. But what is it you seek from me?*

I seek your mercy. Spare his life. Captain Kirk's. Spare the life of my husband. I saved him once, but now it is up to you. Take me instead. I will die with you. But save him. I beg you.

Ola, are you willing to exchange your life for his? the god asked.

No! Kirk cried.

Yes, she said.

But why? cried Ay-nab with astonishment.

Because I love him.

Love? You know of love?

I do, and because of it, I ask you to spare him.

No! Kirk cried again. *Ola, don't do it. He can't . . . he won't . . .* Suddenly Kirk realized that no one could hear him. He was alone. The fire in his mind had vanished. Frantically he cried out, but it was late, far too late.

Kirk was alone in the shell of his mind.

When Kirk awoke, the first thing he saw was the anxious face of Lieutenant Commander Montgomery Scott. He thought it was the most gorgeous sight he had ever witnessed in his life.

"Captain Kirk, thank God!" Scotty cried, seeing Kirk's open eyes. "I thought for sure we'd lost you."

Kirk's head ached. Reaching up, he rubbed the temples, trying to ease the agony. The world around him seemed familiar. He struggled to place it. Sick bay. Yes, that was it. The sick bay of the USS *Enterprise.*

What was he doing here?

"Scotty, what's happened to me?" he said.

"Why, you've been asleep, Captain, that's all. In a few minutes I'm sure you'll be all right."

"But how did I get aboard the ship?"

"You were brought here. The same as the rest of them. Dr. McCoy said you'd pulled a neat trick. He said you'd saved all of our lives."

"But what about the black hole?" Kirk tried to sit up, but Scotty pushed him gently down.

"Don't you worry about that hole," he said. "We're a good long ways distant from it now."

"We are?"

"It's just as I said, sir. We were saved. We're in open space, free at last of that damnable planet."

"You were able to regain control of the engines?"

"No, Captain. It was nothing that simple. One moment we were stuck inside that planet, and the next we were way out here, with everyone back on board. If I wasn't a scientific man, I'd call it magic. Mr. Spock says there's a logical explanation. You'll have to ask him for it."

Even without Spock, Kirk could guess at what must have happened. Ay-nab had decided at last to grant his plea for mercy.

"We were the only ones who were saved," he said.

"No, Captain, the Klingons got out, too. They've been trying to call us, but Mr. Spock says we've got nothing to say to them. I suspect he knows his business."

"And the Lyrans? The natives?"

"Well, Captain, I believe that—"

Scotty never had a chance to finish his thought. A door opened. Kirk turned to see who it was. Dr. Leonard McCoy entered the room, a big happy grin on his face. "Jim, am I ever pleased to see you back among us."

McCoy wasn't alone. A second, smaller figure came tagging after him.

"Ola!" Kirk cried. "You are here."

She smiled shyly. "Yes, Captain Kirk. You have saved my life once again."

"No," he said. "You've got it backward, Ola. It was you who saved me, who saved all of us. Again."

26

A short time ago, accompanied by several of my senior officers, I watched on the bridge viewscreen as an entire inhabited planet disappeared inside a black hole. The event was no more cataclysmic than the snuffing out of a lamp. One moment Lyra floated in space; the next, it had vanished. As to what actually transpired, opinions differ. My chief physicist, Lieutenant Commander Gregory, mentioned several hypotheses. The most intriguing theory holds that black holes may be gateways to other parts of this universe or to entirely separate universes. Naturally, this is only speculation.

I have spoken to Ola concerning her future. Upon the completion of our mission, I intend to take her to the nearest starbase for permanent relocation. Ola says she very much looks forward to finding a new home, an attitude that pleases me. Lieutenant Uhura's recovery continues to proceed at a satisfactory rate. According to Dr. McCoy, she will retain few memories of her ordeal on Lyra.

Shortly after the obliteration of the planet, I accepted a call from Princess Kyanna, who informed me that she would soon be returning home. Once the Klingon ship leaves this area, I intend to follow it at a safe distance. I still have no way of knowing how much of Princess Kyanna's story of treachery

148

and rebellion is true. From her eagerness to return home, I'd guess that most was told me as a lie.

Lying flat on his back in his bunk, James Kirk watched the words whizzing past on the rectangular screen at the foot of his bed and knew that later on he would have to ask the computer for a complete replay; he wasn't following more than every third word. It wasn't the fault of the story. It was just that at the present time he couldn't seem to move his mind far enough from the reality of the moment to plunge effortlessly into the fictional universe of Tolstoy's Russia.

There was a knock at the door. Kirk said, "Come in."

"I hope I'm not disturbing you, Captain," Mr. Spock said, entering diffidently.

Kirk turned in surprise. Spock rarely visited anyone's quarters. "To what do I owe the honor of this visit?"

"It's nothing so dramatic, Captain." Spock shook his head. "I merely felt there were certain matters you and I ought to discuss."

Switching off the computer screen, Kirk waved Spock to a chair. "A particular problem, Mr. Spock?"

"I don't know if I would define it that way. Certain unusual events have recently disturbed me."

"In what fashion, Mr. Spock?"

"In terms of logic."

Kirk nodded. "I thought that's what you were getting at. What you mean to say is that not everything that happened on Lyra has a logical explanation."

"I would have to agree with that, Captain."

"But you're wrong," Kirk said softly. "Everything does. You just have to be willing to accept the concept of a god who is also a star."

"That's just the problem, Captain. You see, I find it very difficult to accept just that."

"Do you have an alternative?"

"I do, although it is only a theory. It is conceivable that the events on Lyra were actually directed by a computer sufficiently advanced that it had developed a legitimate intelligence. For instance, when we first scanned the planet, the sensors failed to detect any life forms capable of intelligence. A highly sophisticated computer might possibly have deflected our signal and concealed the existence of the Lyran village."

"A god might have done that, too. Have you forgotten, Mr. Spock? I spoke with Ay-nab. Can a computer develop a telepathic talent?"

"It is not impossible. A computer built by the same brilliant minds who designed Lyra itself."

"How do you explain our trip through space?"

"A telepathic computer might also possess a telekinetic gift."

"Aren't you reaching rather far for explanations, Mr. Spock?"

"Is it farther than a god who is also a star, Captain?"

"How do you explain the Strangers? Can a computer resurrect the dead?"

"We have no firm proof that these creatures were dead."

"I saw them, Mr. Spock. I fought with one. They were not ordinary beings."

"That does not make them dead, Captain."

Kirk stifled his growing irritation. "Mr. Spock, is this all you have to say? Somehow I get the feeling that you didn't come all the way down here to see me just to find a sounding board for a rather outrageous theory. Is there something else, Mr. Spock? Something new you want to tell me?"

Spock hesitated a long moment before replying. "As you know, my mind is more receptive than yours to telepathic contact."

"I know that, yes."

"Because I am a student of the Vulcan technique of mind touch."

"Yes, yes," Kirk said impatiently.

"A short time ago, while I was standing watch on the bridge, I received a very clear and definite message."

Kirk stared in surprise. "A telepathic message?"

Spock nodded.

"From whom?"

"From someone calling himself Ay-nab."

Kirk barely restrained an urge to smile. "You just got through telling me that Ay-nab doesn't exist."

"I said he might be a highly advanced computer. That isn't the point. Do you want me to relay the message or not?"

"Of course I do."

"It said, 'Tell Captain Kirk that all is well with Ay-nab and his children.'"

"You received that message?"

"With absolute clarity."

"Well, how about that?" Kirk shook his head. *All is well.* What exactly did that mean? He could think of several possibilities, each as bizarre as the next. "Have you told anyone else about this message?" he asked Spock.

"No one."

"Do you think a computer could send a telepathic message from inside a black hole?"

Spock hesitated. "I find that very difficult to accept," he said carefully.

"So do I. But a god?"

Spock spread his hands. "If such entities exist, perhaps one could."

Kirk nodded slowly. "If I were you, Mr. Spock, I don't think I'd mention this to anyone."

"I have no proof that I actually received such a message."

"That's what I mean. It may have been a hallucination."

"Vulcans do not hallucinate, Captain."

"So I've been told, Mr. Spock."

For a long moment neither of them said a word. Minutes passed slowly. Finally Kirk raised his head. "This is an immensely puzzling universe in which you and I live, Mr. Spock."

"But an interesting one."

"What would we do if it ever turned out to be dull?"

Spock shook his head. There was nothing more to say. He glanced at the computer screen. "A game of chess, Captain?"

Kirk nodded firmly and reached out to call the computer. "Chess, it is," he said.

From the author of *The War Against the Chtorr* comes a harrowing space adventure!

UNDER THE
EYE
OF
GOD

David Gerrold

Once they had been humanity's last best hope: a race of genetically engineered killing machines called the Phaestor and their army of deadly Moktar Dragons. Now, the enemy long vanquished, the Phaestor themselves have become the enemy, seizing control of the galaxy and subjugating all lesser species—including humans—to feed their appetite for terror and blood. Now, on a far-flung world, a small group of rebels prepare to strike back against their vampire overlords, bringing revolution to the stars for the only thing worth fighting for: their freedom!

☐ Available at your local bookstore or use this page to order.
☐ Under the Eye of God (29010-X * $5.99/$6.99 Canada)

Send to: Bantam Books, Dept. SF 229
2451 S. Wolf Road
Des Plaines, IL 60018

Please send me the items I have checked above. I am enclosing
$_____ (please add $2.50 to cover postage and handling). Send
check or money order, no cash or C.O.D.'s, please.

Mr./Ms._____

Address_____

City/State_____ Zip_____

Please allow four to six weeks for delivery.
Prices and availability subject to change without notice.

SF 229 12/93

■ *The Jedi Academy Trilogy* ■

Star Wars®

Jedi Search
by Kevin J. Anderson

As the war between the Republic and the remnants of the Empire continues, two children—Jedi twins—will come into their powers in a universe on the brink of vast changes and challenges. In this time of turmoil and discovery, an extraordinary new *Star Wars* saga begins....

While Luke Skywalker takes the first step towards setting up an academy to train a new order of Jedi Knights, Han Solo and Chewbacca are taken prisoner on the planet Kessel. But when Han and Chewie escape, their flight leads to a secret Imperial research laboratory—and from one danger to a far greater one....Luke picks up their trail only to come face-to-face with a weapon so awesome, it can wipe out an entire solar system. It is a death ship called the Sun Crusher, invented by a reclusive genius and piloted by none other than Han himself....

ALIENS™

In space, only *they* can hear you scream....

They come in silence, like death in the night...
They breed inside the living and kill at birth....
Born on another world, they are perfect killing machines....

Based on the spectacular hit movies from Twentieth Century Fox and the bestselling Dark Horse graphic novels, the *Aliens* series chronicles a whole new adventure of terror for the last remnants of humanity! Follow Billie, Wilkes, Ripley, and others as they fight the alien menace in a battle for the possession of Earth.

☐ **Aliens: Earth Hive**

by Steve Perry (56120-0 * $4.99/$5.99 in Canada)

☐ **Aliens: Nightmare Asylum**

by Steve Perry (56158-8 * $4.99/$5.99 in Canada)

☐ **Aliens: The Female War**

by Steve Perry and Stephani Perry
(56159-6 * $4.99/$5.99 in Canada)

☐ **Aliens: Genocide**

by David Bischoff (56371-8 * $4.99/$5.99 in Canada)

Buy all the *Aliens* novels on sale now wherever Bantam Spectra Books are sold, or use this page for ordering.